"Are you free?"

Free? But it had been a one-night stand. Hadn't it? "For what purpose?"

"You want specifics?"

"Sure. Why not?"

When his voice slid through the phone, deep and slow, the vibrations sent tingles all over her skin.

"I was imagining we'd..." He paused. Long enough that she held her breath. "Eat. And later, much later, once I've loosened my tie, and you've kicked your shoes off under the table, and we're both nicely pickled on some excellent wine, together we would do...dessert."

Somehow she managed to keep her voice from cracking when she said, "So you're asking me on a date."

Laughter rolled through the phone. "I'm asking you to eat dinner with me, but if you'd prefer to call it that—"

"Nooo!" *Not a date!*

"No?" he repeated after several long beats.

Caitlyn bit her lip. Dax was a man she'd taken home from a bar. For sex. Not as some kind of Hail Mary that might lead to something more. Her strident rejection of the word *date* had given her an accidental out, if that's what she wanted.

Was it what she wanted?

In her previous life, Australian author **ALLY BLAKE** was at times a cheerleader, a math tutor, a dental assistant and a shop assistant. In this life Ally is a bestselling, multi-award-winning novelist who has been published in more than twenty languages, with over two million books sold worldwide.

She married her gorgeous husband in Las Vegas—no Elvis in sight, though Tony Curtis did put in a special appearance—and now Ally and her family, including three rambunctious toddlers, share a property in the leafy western suburbs of Brisbane, with kookaburras, cockatoos, rainbow lorikeets and the occasional creepy-crawly. When not writing she makes coffees that never get consumed, eats too many M&M's, attempts yoga, devours *The West Wing* reruns, reads every spare minute she can and cheers ardently for the Collingwood Magpies footy team.

You can find out more at her website, www.allyblake.com.

Other titles by Ally Blake available in ebook:

Harlequin Presents® Extra

152—THE ROGUE WEDDING DATE

THE RULES OF ENGAGEMENT

ALLY BLAKE

~ It Starts with a Touch... ~

HARLEQUIN®
entertain, enrich, inspire™

Recycling programs
for this product may
not exist in your area.

ISBN-13: 978-0-373-52896-7

THE RULES OF ENGAGEMENT

Copyright © 2012 by Ally Blake

THE RULES OF
ENGAGEMENT

This one's for fairy dust.
May it sparkle for you, too.

CHAPTER ONE

THE Sand Bar, a cool little club in a tucked-away lane off Melbourne's Chapel Street, was pumping that Saturday night.

'He's cute!' said Franny, shouting to be heard.

Caitlyn played with her sparkly chandelier earrings as she stared dreamily at the buff Cutey Patootey in the T-shirt and jeans at the other end of the bar. 'Isn't he just? And for an outdoorsy-type guy he actually has really nice hands. I'm sure he plays the piano.'

Franny laughed into her cocktail sending the flamingo swizzle-stick spinning. 'If he plays the piano then the doodles on the notepad beside my phone make me the next Picasso.'

Caitlyn dropped her hand to her drink and blinked at Franny. 'Meaning?'

'Only you would see husband potential in a first date.'

'I never! I—'

'You know you do!' Franny said, cutting Caitlyn off. 'You see hearts and flowers, when what you actually need is a guy who can keep you in line. Who doesn't let you get away with the crap you usually do. One who dances to the beat of his own drum, not yours.'

Caitlyn glanced back at Cutey Patootey just as he sucked in his washboard stomach as a pair of bouncy blondes swayed past. Her mouth twitched. 'Believe me, I'm not hearing wedding bells this time.'

Franny gave her a nudge, then out of the corner of her mouth said, 'But have you heard bedsprings creaking?'

Caitlyn smacked her hard on the upper arm. 'We met a week ago.'

Franny shook her head as if that was no kind of answer, which in Frannyland it wasn't.

Caitlyn, on the other hand, wasn't about to jump into bed with some random guy just because he gave her that sweet rush that came from meeting someone new. That had never been her bag. For her, the attraction was all about the delicious slow burn at the beginning of a relationship. The shy glances, and first touches and stolen kisses, and that build of delicious tension 'til they could no longer keep their hands off one another—what a thrill! So much better than the reality that always came later. So Cutey Patootey was going to have to wait.

He glanced back at the girls and grinned; big, brawny, honestly a little less erudite than she might have liked. But Franny was right; with the dimples and spiky blond hair he was ridiculously cute.

With a self-satisfied smile, Caitlyn motioned to Franny she was about to make a beeline for the ladies' room for a freshen up. She sucked in her stomach and ducked and weaved her way through the heaving Saturday night club crowd.

Once through she let out her stomach and craned her neck to see which direction the rest rooms had gone, when she turned and smacked face first into a wall.

At least it felt like a wall. That was until she reached out and grabbed it and discovered it was warm, and slightly yielding, and wearing a suit.

She tried to push off it only to find the crowd pressing at her back.

'Whoa,' she said, half laughing, half hanging on for dear life as she righted herself using the wall as her guide.

And then she looked up. And up. And up.

Dark hair, dark eyes, dark expression. Hello Handsome.

She stood staring into those dark eyes for a long time. Seconds? Minutes?

'So sorry,' she finally said, as breathless as though she'd had the air knocked from her lungs.

Then just when she decided he wasn't going to answer her back, a deep dark velvet voice said, 'Whatever for?'

She swallowed. Tried to anyway. Turned out her mouth had dried up.

Shaking her fringe from her eyes and feigning a confidence that was feeling a tad shaky right about then, she looked right into his eyes, and said, 'I don't make a habit of throwing myself into the arms of passing strangers.'

'Yet you're so good at it.'

She laughed, and her breasts pressed against him. His hard warm chest. She felt a weakening at the backs of her knees. She curled her hands tighter around his lapels.

She wished she could see his eyes better. To see if he was smiling too. The club wasn't exactly dark, but he somehow seemed to swallow the light around him.

'Okay,' she said, 'so it's a move. Not an original one. A classic, really. And I'm sticking by it.'

'Mmm. There's a reason why classics become classics,' he drawled, his rich velvety voice making her shoulders roll as though someone were running a slow finger right down her spine.

'Why's that?'

'They work.'

She could feel the beat of the music in her stomach. Or

perhaps it was her pulse, thumping hard and fast through her centre. Unless it was his pulse. His thumping. They were pressed close enough for it to be possible.

'Caitlyn March,' she said, figuring it impolite to be quite so plastered against the man and not at least introduce herself. She unpeeled a hand to shake his.

'Dax Bainbridge.'

'Nice to meet you.'

'Likewise.'

The house lights flashed at that moment—on off on off—in time with an eighties dance hit and she finally saw his face. Gorgeous didn't even begin to cut it. It was the kind of face she'd have immediately looked away from if caught staring for fear of public drooling.

And then he smiled.

It wasn't a grin by any stretch of the imagination. But the serious cheek creased in the kind of way that set a girl's heart to racing, and the dark eyes gleamed, but it was plenty enough to make Caitlyn feel as if she'd just been clubbed over the back of the head.

Her brain became a fog. She could see the wave and sway of dancing clubbers out of the corner of her eye, and it felt as though they were moving in slow motion. The steady thump of the music pulsed in her stomach. Lower. Boom, boom, boom.

Were the two of them swaying in time with the music now? If not, it felt as if they sure as heck should be.

'Are you a dancer?' she asked. But when she felt him take a breath to answer, she got in first. 'I meant do you get your dance moves on at places like this? Not professionally, of course. I didn't mean you look like a ballerina or anything. And I'm not sure it would be physically possible to achieve head-spins in that suit.'

No response, not that she blamed him. Though his chest

rumbled deliciously against hers. Was he laughing? God, she was literally having to stop herself from breathing the guy in he smelled so delicious, and he was laughing.

She knew she ought to just let him be, to back away slowly and go…wherever it was she'd been planning to go when she stumbled upon him. Where was that again? But he smelled so good, felt so solid, gave her such an array of the most delicious goose bumps, she couldn't.

Literally.

She realised then that his arms were around her. Not inappropriately in any way, shape or form. The song playing was the kind that always had half the nightclub trying to squeeze onto a dance floor three sizes too small and he was merely keeping her from smacking into any other nightclubbers. Or walls for that matter. It was a gentlemanly thing.

She was bumped, jostled, nudged closer. His arms tightened. The crowd moved away. His arm did not. And suddenly it didn't feel so gentlemanly after all.

He shifted his weight. Or maybe she'd shifted hers. Either way when the shifting stopped they were closer again. Her thighs were introduced to the hardness of his. His belt buckle got to know the dent of her belly button. Her blood rushed so hard and fast through her, her head had begun to spin.

She felt as if the floor had dropped out from under her and she was balancing on the edge. Like if the guy moved the wrong way—or more specifically the *right* way—she might leap into his arms, wrap her legs around him and never let go. He was so strong, so warm, he had her wondering if there was a back alley to the place. A hard, private wall up against which he and she could—

And then she remembered the guy at the bar. The guy

with whom she was on a date. Whatshisname? Seriously, what was his name?

Honestly, in the end, it was less that than the fact that her toes had begun to go numb from standing on them in some kind of effort not to feel completely swamped by the man's height that she lowered shakily into her high heels, uncurled her clenched fingers from his jacket, peeled herself from his person, and took a slow and unsteady step away.

The dance song came to a halt. Something slower and softer moaned through the overworked speakers. The strobing lights disappeared and the room was lit with a soft even glow.

'Well, thanks for not letting me fall,' she said, still needing to half shout to be heard.

'Thank you for letting me not let you fall.'

She managed to laugh despite the strange tumbling inside her stomach. Then his cheek did the sexy crease thing again, and she might even have said something like, *Lovely.* But no. She couldn't have. That would be embarrassing along the lines of having her dress caught up in her undies.

She discreetly checked her dress. All good.

'Right.' She flapped her hands over her shoulders in the general direction of the bar. 'I'd better get back to my friend before she thinks I've been abducted by little green men. Not that she's some kind of rabid believer in UFOs, or those kinds of things. Though once, late one night, we did see something odd—'

Stop! Go! Now!

'Okay, then. Bye!' she said.

He acknowledged her with a bow of his head. A small smile. And a glint in his eyes that seemed a hell of a lot like the kind of shockingly hot attraction she was dealing very badly with herself at that very moment.

Caitlyn curtsied. Curtsied! Then stepped back, bumped

into someone, spun on her heel, apologised profusely, smacked another dancer, turned to wave to Dax again so that his final impression of her wasn't her elbowing a stranger in the head, to find he was gone.

She stood a moment in the middle of the dance floor, feeling a little adrift, actually.

When a group of grinning guys in matching 'Pub Crawl' T-shirts surrounded her, she came to quick smart. She ducked under their waving arms and aimed her unsteady feet in the direction of Franny.

As her knees shook she couldn't remember having such an instantaneously intense response to meeting a man in, well, *ever*. All that from a bit of body contact, a smouldering gaze, and a five-minute almost-conversation. No shy glances, and cheeky first touches there. It had felt as if a bomb had gone off inside her. She held a hand to her stomach to quell the lingering ache.

Alas, intensity was the absolute *last* thing she wanted or needed. She'd lived through enough intensity to last her a lifetime during her latest break-up.

George hadn't taken it well, poor love. No wonder, he'd been so sure of her he'd gone so far as to give her his grandmother's engagement ring. But panic had set in, as it inevitably did, and she'd ended it.

She shook it off, literally shimmying away the discomfort of the whole incident, which was draping itself over her like an old shawl that smelled of mothballs. Things were different now. She was different. At least she was trying to be.

At first she'd tried swearing off men for good. But holing up on the couch every Saturday night had sent her nearly around the bend. Now she'd decided, with Franny's encouragement, that what she needed wasn't self-enforced sobriety, just some simple honest-to-goodness fun. A light, easy-going, melt-in-the-mouth kind of guy; sorbet to cleanse her romantic palate.

'What was that?' Franny asked, practically bouncing on the barstool.

Caitlyn slid onto her barstool and feigned fascination for her now lukewarm cocktail. 'What was what?'

'You and the Suit, that's what. I thought you were going to tear one another's clothes off right in the middle of the dance floor. Who is he?'

'Dax…Somebody.'

'Well, Cutey Patootey over there might be a cute *guy*. But that one was all Man.'

Caitlyn glanced at her date to find him sculling beer with the Pub Crawl guys. She winced, and turned back to Franny. 'You say man like it needs a capital M.'

'Go ahead and capitalise the whole word.'

When Franny was quiet for longer than Caitlyn thought possible, she looked up to find her friend staring across the room. Caitlyn couldn't help but follow her lead.

And there he was, Dax…Somebody, standing in a group on the other side of the club. He watched in seeming bemusement as a woman about her age wearing fairy wings was waving her arms at him as if she were about to take off.

Taller than everyone else in sight. Broad too. Dark hair, dark suit. Serious expression. As if he secretly ran the whole world all on his own. As if he always got his way.

Franny was right, he was all Man. Caitlyn breathed in deep through her nose, looking for and finding the tang of his scent, which still lingered on her skin. And just like that the vibration was back, fizzing as potently inside her as it had the moment she'd recognised the heat in his eyes as a direct mirror of hers.

But no matter how much her body was telling her yes, her head knew he was too much for her. All that intensity and heat was a banquet when all she could stomach right then was sorbet.

Pity.

Dax…Somebody discreetly checked his watch, then glanced about the room, his gaze almost colliding with hers.

Cheeks as red and hot as sun-ripened tomatoes, Caitlyn spun away and grabbed Franny by the arm, pulling her friend from a trance.

'Stop staring,' Caitlyn hissed as though he might hear her. 'You'll get RSI.'

'It'll be worth it.'

It was after two a.m. at the hazy, noisy, malodorous nightclub when Dax decided he'd put in an appropriate amount of time at his sister Lauren's birthday bash and was quietly working out the fastest route to the door.

His time was rarely his own. He still had a half dozen endowment proposals to which he needed to give the final stamp of approval and foreign markets to check before he could even think about sleep.

But his feet refused to budge. They were fixed to the floor as if they'd been bolted there, and it had nothing to do with the sticky remnants of a night's worth of spilt booze. He only had a certain someone with dreamy brown eyes to blame.

Dreamy brown eyes that locked on and didn't let go. And warm skin that had felt like velvet beneath his hands. Then there was that mouth. A soft pink mouth that was made for being kissed, and thoroughly.

Caitlyn…*Something*. Even her name had him shifting in his shoes. Shoes that remained stuck, while his eyes began to rove.

The crowd of loose sweaty bodies rolling with the

beat of some obscure song shifted and swayed, revealing glimpses of faraway corners of the club, before swallowing them up in the writhing mass once more.

Dax ran a hand hard and fast up the back of his head, attempting to shake loose the tension coiling through him. A glimpse was all he wanted. A flash of auburn hair and pale skin and warm curves, a memory to take home to his empty bed.

The crowd parted. And there she was. Perched on a stool at the bar. Hair shimmering in the down lights, legs crossed, high heel bouncing up and down, shoulders bare in that so-sweet-it-was-sexy little dress.

The next thing he noticed was the other half-dozen pairs of male eyes zeroed her way. Seedy eyes with one thing on the minds behind them. How a woman like her expected to make it out of a place like that alive was anyone's guess.

Perhaps he ought to make sure she did. Now that he knew her name he felt a kind of responsibility over her. Especially when he knew how much trouble that brazen little mouth of hers could get her into.

That mouth...

His suit began to feel too snug. Too hot. He shifted uncomfortably but it didn't help. If he was honest with himself he knew there was only one thing that would.

He'd never liked loose ends. Never believed some things were better left unsaid. If he wanted any kind of legacy it would be that he was a man who always finished what he started.

His shoes unstuck and he set off—

'Man, you look like you have fleas,' Rob, Lauren's husband, said as he clapped a hand on Dax's shoulder, yanking him back onto his heels.

Dax breathed out hard through his nostrils like a racehorse locked into the starting gate.

'Or an itch needs scratching,' Rob said, motioning towards the bar. Towards her. 'Saw you two out there dancing before. Who is she?'

Caitlyn. Again her name slid through his mind like a siren song. He shoved his hand into the pockets of his suit trousers and levelled his gaze at his brother-in-law. 'There was no dancing, merely a great deal of crowd jostling, and I made sure the lady didn't get trampled.'

'Right,' Rob said, a grin spreading across his face. 'Jostling.'

Dax realised too late that knowing who Rob was talking about had been his big mistake. He dragged his eyes back to the dance floor. 'It was quite a crowd.'

'Or quite a girl.'

Quite a girl? At the mere thought of the end result of the crowd-jostling, heat broke through him like a wildfire with a forest full of dry scrub in its path. Dax sought out a bunch of leg hairs and tugged, but it was to no avail.

Brutal honesty was.

She was a girl who clearly had a defective self-defence mechanism if the way she'd melted against him, a complete stranger, was anything to go by. She'd do better with the nice guy, the Robs of the world, not a hard-headed realist like him, despite the sexual attraction they no doubt shared.

It wasn't enough to warrant pursuit. Especially when he knew nothing about her apart from the fact that she could get his blood boiling with a mere glance. The Bainbridge name brought with it certain advantages. But those same advantages attracted elements best left alone.

His eyes sought out Lauren, who was laughing and dancing. She'd been so young at the time of their parents' accident. So disorientated by the avalanche of chaos they'd left behind and therefore a perfect target to the sharks who'd smelled blood in the water.

It felt so long ago now; he twenty-two, and saddled with not only a shell-shocked sixteen-year-old sister he'd barely known but the rotting carcass of his family's hundred-year-old business. The future he'd imagined for himself gone in a puff of smoke.

He coughed, the haze before his eyes for real. Someone had gone overboard with the club's smoke machine. Through the smog his eyes disobediently sought out the shapely outline of an auburn-haired spitfire.

His self-preservation instincts had been well honed. They'd had to be. Never again would he be as unsuspecting, as stunned to the very core, as he had been by the selfish and systematic fraud his parents had perpetrated so slyly before their deaths.

Though if Caitlyn was a shark in damsel's clothing then he'd change his name to Susan.

Unlike plenty before her, she hadn't looked at him as if he was the answer to her girlhood dreams of diamonds and furs. More like she was a diagnosed sweetaholic and he was the biggest doughnut she'd ever seen.

He felt hot, he felt tight, he felt wide awake. As turn-ons went it appeared her particular brand of upfront, in-your-face, sexual frankness was it.

Could he? Should he?

He glanced at his watch and frowned, unsure if that one move had been a mistake, or his saving grace. It was nearing half-past two. He had work to do. And it had been a long time since his time had been his own.

'Right, I'm off,' Dax said, overly loud to his own ears though the vigour was likely lost in the thump of the booming beat.

He patted Rob hard on the back and searched out his sister. He found her bouncing from one foot to the other, the antenna on her head and fairy wings on her back bobbing right along with her.

'Hey, brother! Don't tell me you're off.'

'I'm afraid I must. I have a conference call at six.'

'So stay 'til then. Get your dancing feet on.' She did a solo tango to illustrate.

'Alas I left my tap shoes in my other car.'

Tango done, she levelled him with a stare. 'At least promise me you had fun?'

'More than I can possibly say.' Having a nubile redhead wrapped about him a definite highlight, though he knew better than to let Lauren in on that score.

'Fine,' she said, sighing dramatically. 'Go. Get your beauty sleep. It wouldn't behove you, or the foundation, if you appeared anything less than implacable.'

After blowing him a kiss, she shimmied and boogied away into the crowd. Whatever things he might wish to change about his past, bringing her up wasn't one of them.

Dax resisted the urge to look towards the bar one last time and turned towards the exit.

Something slithered down his neck. It felt as if it had legs long enough to belong to a bird-eating spider, so he flapped his suit jacket madly 'til whatever it was either flew away or was summarily squished.

He took a step, only to feel his foot slipping out from under him. He caught himself just in time, took a moment to find his breath, then lifted his shoe to find something twinkling at him from the dark wooden floor.

Braving the possibility of disease by letting his fingers stray that close to the layer of sticky ooze, Dax bent to pick it up.

It was long. It was shiny. And it was no bird-eating spider.

* * *

'What are you doing?' Franny asked. 'The cab's waiting.'

Caitlyn, who was at that moment on her hands and knees—with paper napkins keeping all four from actually touching the precarious Sand Bar floor—blew a strand of hair from her mouth. 'I've lost an earring.'

Franny threw out her hands in supplication. 'It could be anywhere by now!'

'Which is why I need to get a move on looking for it.' With a shiver Caitlyn flicked a stray piece of random cocktail fruit from her wrist. 'They were Gran's. The chandeliers with the little flowers at the clasp.'

'Oh,' Franny said, looking suitably understanding. She knew the history those earrings had. Still she glanced longingly towards the door where the guy she'd spent half the last hour dirty dancing with was waiting to take her to heaven and back.

They'd promised to drop Caitlyn home on the way as her lift had evaporated once Cutey Patootey was no longer around to escort her. He'd disappeared into the wee hours after Caitlyn had made it clear, by not letting him stick his tongue in her ear, that she wasn't going home with him that evening.

Caitlyn wasn't all that disappointed. Not about that. Her gran's earrings on the other hand… They meant something deeply. Her heart clenched hard at the thought of losing them for ever.

'You go,' she said, giving Franny a shove on the ankle, which was the only part she could reach from the floor. 'I could be a while.'

Franny bit her lip, looked from Caitlyn's no doubt pathetic position and back to the brooding blond in the leather jacket lounging mysteriously by the door.

'Go!'

'All right!' Franny blushed furiously, then leant over

the bar, getting the attention of the bartender. 'Ivan! See to it our mate Cait makes it safely to a cab all right? And if anyone hands in an earring, it's hers.'

Ivan peered at Caitlyn, grinned and nodded.

Franny said, 'I won't be home tonight. Usual place tomorrow for a warm down?'

'If I must.'

Franny grinned, and took off at a sprint.

Caitlyn spent the next ten minutes peering at the floor and getting nowhere. Every minute down there had felt like an hour and the further she got, the more concerned she became.

She and her dad had picked out those earrings for her gran when she was eleven years old. No matter how short a stay he'd had at home between tours, he'd always made time for just the two of them, but she remembered *that* trip to the shops with him with such clarity. The next time he'd gone on tour he'd never come back.

Something glinted at her under a barstool! She pulled to a crouch, tucked herself into ball, peered underneath and—

'Cait?'

At Ivan's unexpected call, Caitlyn looked up so fast she bumped her head on the underside of the stool. Biting her lip to keep from swearing like a sailor, she rubbed her head and frowned up at him, only to find him holding a long glinting earring made of a dozen pieces of cut glass with a flower at the clasp.

She scrambled most ungracefully to her feet and grabbed the earring and held it to her chest, spinning around so that her hair slapped her in the face, but she didn't care. 'Oh, Ivan! My dear darling Ivan! I love you more than you could ever know!'

'Love *him*,' Ivan said with a grin, cocking his head to the right. 'He found it.'

Caitlyn spun to a halt, spat a clump of hair from her mouth, and found herself looking into a pair of familiar dark eyes.

'Dax,' she said, his name a breathy sigh upon her lips.

Up close and personal he'd been impressive. At enough distance to get a load of the whole lot of him in one go he was…breathtaking. Dark, serious, cool, and with a face that got a girl to thinking she was wearing far too many clothes for comfort.

He seemed not to notice the feminine tremblings she'd resorted to, thank goodness. He just leaned comfortably against the bar, looking as if he'd been standing there watching her shuffle about on her hands and knees for some time and had been perfectly happy to do so.

'*You* found it?' she asked, somewhat redundantly. Though she was pretty impressed she'd been able to get any intelligible words out at all, considering the loudness of the pounding of her pulse in her ears.

'I stood on it,' he said, his deep voice reverberating inside her so that she might as well have been hollow. 'If not for my natural grace you and your earring might have single-handedly laid me flat on my back.'

Dax, flat on his back. The image *that* created was a keeper. One she knew she'd be trotting out on long, cold, lonely winter nights.

'It must have come loose when we…met.' The guy made the word 'met' sound like a dirty word. Good dirty. Behind-closed-doors dirty.

Dax nodded to Ivan, who seemed to understand whatever signal he'd sent and moved away.

Something made Caitlyn almost call out for Ivan to stay. As if being left alone with this man without the aid of loud music, a tightly packed crowd, and low lighting was a kind of peril she knew she couldn't withstand alone.

Dax pushed away from the bar and moved closer. Caitlyn curled her toes so as not to sway away. Even in her high heels she had to tilt her head to maintain eye contact.

He reached out and took her hand. Caitlyn's breath caught in her throat. Then he turned her hand over and uncurled her fingers one by one.

Her gran's gorgeously gaudy earring glinted back at her.

Relief poured through her, partly because she remembered why *he* was really there; not for some random seduction scene, but to return her lost property.

She took a deep breath, centred herself as best she could with his warm male scent curling about her, and turned the earring over in her now moist palm.

'Is it okay?' he asked.

The bar at the back was slightly bent, but other than that it was in perfect nick. 'You're light on your feet for a guy of your size. You could have mashed it completely. She's barely bruised and with a little TLC she'll be as good as gold.'

She risked looking at him. Her eyes locked to his. Hazel. Her new favourite colour in the whole world. Her breath came hard, for there was no hiding from the patent desire in his gaze. Desire for her.

The house lights slowly lifted, encouraging the dregs to stumble on home. Panic set in. Her hair would be a mess, her lipstick bitten away, her mascara ever so delightfully smudged. Yet his expression didn't change. The glint in his eyes if anything grew. Scorched.

OH, GOD!

And for a girl who in the past had lived for the adrenalin brought on by the mere possibility of a new relationship, she felt as if she were free falling into those hot hazel eyes.

In the past being the most important part. She wasn't looking for that brand of blistering intensity that could sweep a girl off her feet before she knew what was happening. She wanted fun and frivolity. She needed…

Sorbet.

All of a sudden parts of herself began to click and slide, like the tumbling open of a combination lock.

What she needed most was emotional catharsis.

What she wanted was to clear the bad taste in her mouth that her most recent failed engagement had left behind.

Sorbet sex.

What kind of sorbet sex she couldn't be certain, since it was her first time going down that route. Sorbet came in a million different flavours, and if hers came in the guise of a tall, dark, handsome stranger she had no doubt could wipe away the memory of every man she'd ever met, well, then, who was she to argue?

'Closing time,' Ivan called out, dragging Caitlyn to the present.

Her breath shook as she wondered how exactly one went about picking up a sexy stranger in a bar by asking for no-strings sorbet sex.

'Hungry?' she asked, before she even felt the word coming.

'Ravenous,' Dax said without missing a single beat.

Well, she thought as he slid his hand around her waist, resting it possessively on her hip as he led her towards the door, even that gentle touch making her feel as if lava were sliding through her veins, *that's how*.

CHAPTER TWO

CAITLYN stood in the long hall outside her apartment, hand shaking as she tried to slide her key into the door. It didn't help that Dax was right behind her, his body heat doing crazy things to her nerves.

They hadn't said a word after piling into the back seat of a taxi, where Caitlyn had barked out her address in a voice that made her sound as if she were impersonating a seal with laryngitis.

Their knees had almost bumped as the taxi rounded each corner, but not. Little fingers had almost touched on the rough fabric seat, but not. Gazes had clashed as they'd sought one another out again and again, threatening to entangle in such a way that had made Caitlyn's heart feel as if it were about to burst from her chest, but not.

By the time they'd reached her South Yarra apartment block Caitlyn was so wired she was amazed she could walk in a straight line.

'Let me,' Dax's deep voice rumbled behind her. He reached around, pried the key from her claw, and slid it into the lock as if the little hussy had just opened up for him with an easy sigh.

Any pretence at actual food being on offer went out the window when with a sigh Caitlyn spun in Dax's arms, slid her hands into his gorgeous hair, pressed as high onto her tiptoes as humanly possible and kissed him for all she was worth.

Postponing gratification as she'd done so many times before had clearly been ass backwards. She'd had barely two conversations with the guy, didn't even remember his last name, and had never been kissed so thoroughly in her whole life.

He was a pro, or at the very least gifted beyond the constraints of natural law. He did things with his tongue she hadn't even imagined were possible. Her body didn't care what was possible or not, it just melted and ached and craved all that and more. More than she possibly knew how to handle.

The intensity brought with it an ache that seemed to fill her very bones, leaving her feeling breathless, and wild with abandon.

Sorbet! she shouted in her head like a mantra when sense threatened to rear its unhelpful head. That was what he was. Sharp, cool, cleansing sorbet. And if by some alignment of the stars he'd had reason to choose her for a one-time thing right when she needed it most, then so be it.

His lips moved to the soft dent below her ear. To the shallow dip at the base of her neck. Nipping along the edge of her collarbone.

Her hands dug into the soft springy hair at the back of his neck, her teeth biting down on her lower lip. Every sense bar the places her body touched his had become so woolly she could no longer feel her extremities.

She only realised that his balance was affected too when they stumbled backwards and the doorknob, key still inside, wedged into her back.

That was when she realised they were *still* in the hall.

Unknown strength rose up within her and somehow she reached behind her, shoved the door open so hard it was a miracle the doorknob stayed on, and grabbed Dax by the lapels to yank him inside. The door shut behind him, plunging them into darkness. Only a thin vertical stripe of light peeked through the edge of the lounge-room curtains.

They stilled, her fingers curled into his suit jacket, his hot breaths lifting the hair from her shoulders.

The lack of sight made everything suddenly magnified. The whir and clank of her old fridge turning to life. The distant hum of riverside traffic below throbbing in time with her heart.

At the slow, deliberate slide of his hand as it found a happy place in the small of her back, her skin prickled and burned. She pressed deliciously into the hard plancs of his body.

And as his lips landed upon hers, insistent and hot as hell, every sound near and far slipped away on a tide of liquid warmth.

He lost his jacket along the way, and his tie. She hoped her shoes had made it inside the apartment but she wasn't quite sure. All she knew was an almost primal need to get horizontal.

They tumbled backwards through the dark apartment, bumping into couches, lamp tables, a fake potted plant. The folded edge of a twist pile rug almost tripped her up completely.

When something wobbled off some surface and crashed, Dax jerked in surprise, but Caitlyn just grabbed him by the chin and kissed him harder.

Not needing to be told twice, he wrapped his arms around her, lifted her bodily off the floor and found the way to her bedroom without bumping into anything, as though he had some kind of sexual GPS built in.

The moonlight pouring through the sheer curtains at her bedroom window was oh, so thankfully brighter, giving her a perfect view of Dax's supreme male body. His shirt and trousers were gone leaving him in black cotton boxers. She felt herself smiling at how conservative his underwear was considering what they were about to do. Then he breathed deep through his nose, like a stallion sensing a mare in heat, and took a step her way and what they were about to do took precedence over every other thought.

He found the zip of her little cocktail dress, lowered it slowly, and her vertebrae collapsed in upon themselves in empathy.

Clothes off, protection on, the backs of her knees found the edge of her bed and she sank back, he moved with her. Big, strong, firm, confident, and heartbreakingly beautiful.

Only he would not be breaking her heart. And she would most definitely not break his. As though that was the final permission she needed she reached up, slid her hand behind his neck and pulled him down to kiss her.

The slip and slide of skin on skin made her breathless, as if her body couldn't process both oxygen and the mad tumble of sensations pummelling her at the same time. Maybe it was the heretofore untried naughtiness of a one-night stand. Maybe because it was a one-time deal she'd given herself permission to just let go.

Maybe it was Dax.

Then he was inside her. It was sudden, shocking, but she was more than ready. Her legs wrapped around him, she needed the feeling intensifying inside her more than she'd known she could. As if this was what she'd been waiting for her whole life. Not that romantic mushy stuff she'd lived on, but *this*.

His lips created havoc wherever they touched, ravaging

her to the point of bonelessness. Making her feel defence-less, vulnerable—

No! This was about her taking back control over her emotional life.

Finding a last vestige of strength, she spun him around until she was on top. His hands found her hips, his thumbs sliding across her hipbone, the tremors shuddering through her all but cutting off any kind of ascendancy she might have had.

She ran her fingernails down his chest, over the solid undulation of slick brown skin. And when his desire-filled eyes closed, and he needed to open his mouth to take in enough breath, she felt formidable. Renewed.

Sensations built, cutting off all thought and feeling bar the desire flooding through her, hot and relentless.

Then all sensation contracted to the size of a pin-head. To some tiny point deep in her core. As swirls of blood-red heat crashed through her mind, through her body, bombarding her senses with more pleasure than she could process, the only vaguely coherent thought was that in her whole short life she'd never known it could feel like that.

Never.

This from the first guy she'd ever looked at and said, *This is a one-time deal.*

Frankly, considering why she'd gone looking for sorbet sex in the first place, it was more than she deserved.

Caitlyn sat back in the big leather chair, eyes closed as it hummed blissfully beneath her. A thump to her right told her Franny had finally arrived at their regular Sunday morning date at the Shangri-Lovely Nail Bar.

'Good morning, sunshine!' Caitlyn bubbled.

'How could you start without me?' Franny grumbled.

Caitlyn opened her eyes to find Franny hunched down

in dark sunglasses, her hair pulled back into a scraggy ponytail, grunting as she jabbed in her favourite settings on the massage chair. 'You weren't even home when I left; I thought I might have to go solo today.'

Franny gave a double thumbs-up to her usual pedicurist indicating a double espresso, in a mug, before glancing pointedly at the half-eaten packet of biscuits Caitlyn had resting atop the glossy magazine she hadn't yet found a chance between daydreams to open.

'Chocolate chip? At this time of the morning? It's not as though you worked up an appetite after I left.' Her eyes swung slowly back to Caitlyn. 'Or did you?'

Caitlyn licked a smudge of chocolate from her finger, images of the night before skipping and tripping through her mind like an old silent film. A slideshow of muscled arms, and broad shoulders, and acres of beautiful warm skin turning red beneath her grasping fingernails as she—

A hot flush landed hard and fast upon her cheeks. 'Don't change the subject. We're here to talk about you and the Leather Jacket.'

But Franny was pointing at the pretty pink polish the pedicurist was sliding onto Caitlyn's toenails. 'Look! You did! You got lucky, you dog!'

'What on earth does my toenail polish have to do with anything?'

'All last week you were red. Sex-starved, man-eater red. And today you pick this tiptoeing-through-daisies pink? Something happened between last night and this morning.'

Caitlyn blinked, stumped that she'd given herself away so easily. 'Moody-looking dude in leather jacket first.'

'Fine. As it turns out all that bad-ass leather stopped at the door. His name's Eugene and he lives with his mother. They breed ferrets. Inside the lounge room. None of which I realised until I did the walk of shame this morning. Past his mum. Who had folded my clothes into a neat pile on the chesterfield in the lounge room—'

Franny waved both hands madly over her face. 'I just want to forget the whole thing. Now. Your turn. Did Cutey Patootey come back?'

'No-o-o!'

'Who, then? Not Ivan?'

'The bartender?' For that Franny deserved no more than a blank stare.

Franny frowned, clearly stumped.

Caitlyn hoped she'd stay that way. Hoped she could hang onto the mild buzz she was still wearing like a cloud of exotic perfume all those hours later a little longer before Franny dissected it to death.

Then Franny's foggy morning-after eyes focused fully for the first time.

'The Suit! You hooked up with the Suit! You sly dog!' Franny squealed loud enough the traffic outside the salon would have heard every word.

'Shh. I'm sure everyone else here could care less about the intimate details of my nightscapades.'

Franny glanced around. 'Are you kidding me? Why else do you think women come to places like this? It's hardly rocket science to slap on a dash of nail polish at home. Details. Please. Before I give up men for good.'

Franny leant so far forward on her chair she almost landed in the tub of water at her feet. Her pedicurist arrived in time, shoved her feet in the water and gave her a quelling stare. Franny looked dutifully chastised. 'So who is he? Did he live up to all that glorious potential? Are you seeing him again?'

Caitlyn breathed out long and slow. She wasn't going to get a moment's peace until she gave Franny *something*. Then, staring hard at her toes, she said, 'Fine. His name was Dax. Dax Something Starting With B. Banner? Bale? He looks even better out of the suit than in it. And, no, we didn't make plans to catch up again. Happy?'

Franny grinned as she shook her head and slipped her smart phone from her purse and plugged in a few letters. 'Dax Something Starting With B? Miss March, you sit there with your cute freckles on your little nose looking like butter wouldn't melt in your mouth, but you are so full of surprises.'

Caitlyn knew exactly what she was about to do. She tried to grab the phone but Franny was quicker than she looked.

'Still!' her pedicurist demanded.

'This is *important*,' Franny said, glaring right on back.

The pedicurist shrugged and set to sloughing away the dead skin on Franny's soles.

'Please don't Google the guy, for Pete's sake!' Caitlyn begged.

Franny snorted. 'Are you kidding me? In this day and age it's the first thing you should do the second you learn a guy's name. Heck, if I'd been smart enough to Google Mr Lame from last night I'd have avoided ever knowing what ferret poo smells like. Trust me. I'm doing you a favour.'

Caitlyn set her teeth and stared blindly at the small golden cat with its bobbing head on the cashier's counter. She knew trying to stop Franny was a waste of time. And while she knew it was unlikely she'd ever see the guy again, no small part of her did wonder how a guy who looked like that, and kissed like that, and who'd learnt how to do the things he'd done to her the night before, had managed to get so far in life without being hogtied and hitched at gunpoint.

When Franny had been quiet for all too long Caitlyn glanced at her to find her eyes growing larger and larger until they looked as if they were about to pop out of her head.

'I knew it!' Franny blurted.

'What?' Caitlyn asked despite herself. 'He's married. Of course he's married. Oh, God. How could I have been so—?'

'He's not married.'

Caitlyn's rant came to a halt. The relief flowing through her was totally misguided. Especially since it wasn't relief that he hadn't cheated on his non-existent wife. It was relief that he was actually on the market.

She wasn't. Sure it had been six months since she'd broken up with George. Not just broken up, she reminded herself, called off her engagement. But she was done with all that: relationships, and dating, and blah blah blah.

Yet she found herself leaning towards Franny and saying, 'Then what?'

'Your Dax Something Starting With B was Dax Bainbridge, as in CEO of the Bainbridge Foundation. Heard of them?'

Caitlyn blinked. Several times. '*Them* yes. A representative of the Bainbridge Foundation is a no-brainer on *any* launch list, though they never accept. They're less A-list party-hard types, more old money, right?'

'You should know your guest lists better.'

Caitlyn crossed her arms. 'I know everyone who buys sports cars, and everyone who wishes they could buy sports cars. Everyone else is a blur.'

Franny eyeballed her. 'You're really sitting there and saying this guy is a blur?' Franny turned her phone around and shoved it at her. And Caitlyn found herself staring at a picture of the man who'd driven her wild in bed the night before.

Dark hair, straight eyebrows, hooded hazel eyes, a haughty nose straight out of a Jane Austen novel, a jaw line that would have sent Michelangelo shopping for marble. God, he really was as gorgeous as she remembered him.

Her hormones went on such a sudden spree it caused her

heart to leap into her throat and stay there. If she'd been wearing a tie she would have loosened it.

Franny shoved her phone into her massive bag, apologising to her pedicurist with a smile for having dared move. 'His place?' she asked.

'Ours.'

'Of course. Home-ground advantage.'

Franny probably didn't know how right she was. The thought of having to creep out of bed and get dressed in the same clothes as the night before would have put her in far too fragile a position, and the night before had been about getting control back over her life. Her place had been the right place for sorbet sex. She couldn't get any funny ideas about possible permanence if it was up to her to kick the guy out.

'So is he the next almost Mrs Caitlyn March?'

Caitlyn shook her head so hard it hurt. 'It was—'

Exhilarating, euphoric, erotic, she thought.

What she said was, 'It was a one-time deal.'

'Good,' Franny said. 'For the best if it stays that way.'

Caitlyn nodded absent-mindedly as her leather massage chair began its sequence of thumping rolls down her back.

They'd had that same discussion a dozen or more times in the weeks since poor George's ignominious departure from their lives. Franny had even come up with a mantra she was sure Caitlyn ought to have stamped on her forehead, at least for the next little while: *Men can be for fun, not only for for ever.*

Which was partly why she didn't tell Franny that at the last second she'd given Dax her number, scribbling it down on the back of a grocery receipt and shoving it into his jacket pocket as they'd made out like teenagers in her apartment doorway at some ungodly hour of the morning.

'Stop,' Franny said.

The pedicurist looked up with a frown. Franny rolled her eyes at her before pointing a thumb at Caitlyn. The pedicurist gave her a knowing nod before heading back to her manic buffing.

'Stop thinking about him. It's dangerous.'

'Are you kidding me? I can't move without being reminded of my midnight acrobatics,' she said out of the corner of her mouth. 'I can still smell his cologne on my hair. Trust me, it's not that easy to just turn it off.'

Franny spun on her big massage chair and looked Caitlyn in the eye, grabbing her by both hands. This time the pedicurist didn't complain. She looked up at Caitlyn too, eyes questioning, buffer poised over Franny's toes.

'Cait, my sweet,' Franny said, 'listen to me this once. You don't smoke. The hardest drug I've ever seen you take is really strong caffeine. You don't pick your nose in public. But your one true vice is romance. You get so caught up in it I could dance naked in front of you right now and you wouldn't see it for the stars in your eyes. You, my friend, are addicted to love. It's your one and only failing. But as failings go it has potential to be a doozie. It's a failing that can and has dragged chaos and catastrophe in its wake.'

Caitlyn squeezed Franny's hand. 'I can handle this. He's not… It was nothing like the others. I promise.'

'If you say so.' With that Franny slid on her dark sunglasses and proceeded to fall asleep in her chair.

The pedicurist shrugged, clearly disappointed, and got back to work.

While Caitlyn picked up her magazine, and pretended to read it while the words chaos and catastrophe swam in front of her eyes. That and the look on George's face when she'd tried to give back the ring. No shock. No anger. Just resignation, as if he'd seen it coming before she had. Her chest compressed, masking for a moment Dax's spicy scent lingering on her skin.

Because the truth was, George wasn't her first.

Caitlyn had been engaged more than once.

Three times in fact.

Franny might have thought it an endearing character quirk, but she was probably the only one. Caitlyn was fairly sure her mother thought her a strumpet, and that was when she wasn't thinking her a grave disappointment. Not that she'd ever been given a hint as to what she could have done right on that score.

She shook off the sense of dejection her mother's particular lack of affection had always engendered. If ever she needed a trigger to send her running into the arms of the first guy who smiled her way, her mum's cold shoulder was a good one.

Sometimes that was all it took—a sexy smile, a second glance, a fleeting nod across a crowded bar—and suddenly weeks had gone by and she was hurtling along the same old path. High on the rush of feeling adored.

And if someone adored her enough to ask her to *marry* them? God… Was there any way to feel more cherished?

Problem was, that was when she realised the view from the top wasn't what she'd imagined it would be. And there was no way to go but down, the weight of a ring hanging uncomfortably on her finger making the descent all the faster.

Caitlyn flipped the magazine shut and closed her eyes, wriggling her toes under the fan drying her toenail polish as she tried to take the edge off the chill that had wrapped itself around her.

That little bit of heat was enough to rip her from the highs and lows of her past and right smack bang into last night.

To *Dax*. His name shifted through her on a heady sigh.

Everything about Dax had been different. He hadn't looked at her once as if she was all his dreams come true. He was assertive. Yet elusive. All outer cool and inner heat.

She wriggled in her chair as the familiar slip and slide of desire began to sizzle inside her. Whoever said you needed to love a guy to enjoy sex had either never had great sex with a stranger before, or was justly using the myth to convince teenage girls of that fact.

And by jumping straight into bed with him she'd missed some of the most addictive steps in the process—the long walks holding hands, the casual touches that heralded so much more, all the intimate stuff she seemed to mistake for love every time.

Did that mean she had a string of one-night stands with random guys to look forward to in her future?

She scrunched up her nose and decided not to think about how disquieted that made her feel. Better to just enjoy the gorgeous warm loose feeling she'd been indulging all morning.

She'd earned it. For she was on the right track to not getting caught in the same emotional trap again.

Dax tossed a Berocca into a glass of water—his third of the day. As he watched the orange tablet fizzing giddily to the bottom of the glass as it dissolved he ran a hand up the back of his neck, 'til his fingers hit hard plastic.

He took off the baseball cap and held it in his hands, bending the brim. He couldn't remember the last time he'd gone into the office in jeans and a baseball cap. If ever.

What had Lauren said? Something about him never wanting to appear anything less than implacable?

If so it was only because he knew he needed to exude confidence and above all trust. They needed to trust he could do the job. Those qualities that the Bainbridge name alone had once evoked he'd had to work damn hard to re-kindle after his parents had thrown it all away in the name of hard and fast living.

But the thought of throwing on a suit that Sunday morning and controlling the unruly spikes of his hair had been beyond even him.

He'd yet to go to sleep. How could he? Every time he'd closed his eyes he'd been bombarded with images of a lissom redhead. Her head falling back, gasping for breath as she closed tight around him. Then the dense blur that had set in around him before scattering to the very edges of his consciousness, taking with it every thought, every 'to do' list, every agenda until all was quiet for a moment. Which was a moment more than he'd had in a long time.

The clouds outside his tenth-storey window parted, sending a shaft of painfully bright spring sunshine right onto the papers scattered across his desk, the whiteness giving him an instant headache. He closed his eyes and skulled the fizzy drink, wiping away with it all thoughts of the night before.

There were papers he had to get a handle on before open of business Monday. Memos from a forensic accountant he'd hired on a hunch that so far did not herald good news. Far from it. He might have been blind to the depths of his parents' transgressions, but his instincts had never seen him wrong since.

If following those instincts meant putting aside far more pleasant thoughts in order to maintain the distinction of credibility, then that was what he'd do.

Implacable? He'd been called far worse, but that was what the foundation had needed when he'd been forced to take it over. The choice then had been ruthlessness or ruin.

The success he'd wrested from near-disaster had given him no reason, no chance, no option, to change.

He slid the cap back onto his head, the narrow brim thankfully blocking out the harshest hit of sunlight.

When there was work to be done, daydreams of sweet-lipped redheads would simply have to wait their turn, along with everything else in his life.

Caitlyn's excuse for spending way too much time on the factory floor Monday morning was that she was in charge of throwing a massive bash to launch the product kept under tight wraps down there. The fact that it also meant she had the opportunity to drool over the first Pegasus Z9 sports car fresh off the production line might have had a little to do with it too.

Like something out of an original James Bond movie, the Z9 was all soft leather interior, glinting spoked wheels, warm deep-set headlights, and curves luscious enough to take on the most buxom cheesecake pin-up of the same era.

It was beautiful, brilliant and built to last, just as anything well designed ought to be.

'Honestly, Doug,' she said to the mechanical engineer who, computer tablet in hand, was giving his beloved creation the third once-over that day, 'she's delectable. The second sexiest thing I've seen all year.'

Doug's bushy red eyebrows rose in question.

Caitlyn grinned. 'It's been quite a week.'

Doug glanced at her hands for about the eighth time, making sure she wore the requisite white cotton gloves, and then he went back to the object of his desire, leaving Caitlyn free to daydream at leisure about hers.

She ran a gloved finger over the voluptuously rounded fender of the Z9 until her fingers tingled with the sense memory of springy dark hair sliding through them and she had to bite her fingertips into her palms to stop from moaning out loud.

She'd had to have gone and given Dax her phone number, hadn't she? Rookie mistake. One she ought not to be punishing herself for, except she kept jumping out of her skin every time her phone rang.

He probably wouldn't call at all. Probably didn't have the time. According to those in the know, and Wikipedia, he was something of a workaholic corporate wunderkind who'd taken over the family biz when his parents died in a light plane crash in Aspen or some such rich person playground.

But if he *did* call, she wondered when that might be. Midweek? Weekend? In Franny's considered opinion the difference between those two times told a girl everything. Midweek meant date. End of the week meant booty call. If that was true then it was certainly in Caitlyn's best interest to just stop thinking about it any more until Friday—

Her phone shrilled in her back pocket. Pulling off the gloves, she drew it out between two fingers, as if it might burn, only to find a private number on the display. Likely press. They liked to get the jump on people.

Nevertheless her voice was husky when she answered with a distracted, 'Caitlyn March.'

'Good morning,' said the deep male voice that had been whispering sweet nothings in her imagination all morning.

Caitlyn's knees gave way and luckily the Z9 was at hand. She grabbed the side mirror so as not to land on her backside. Doug frowned at her. She quickly let go, wiped off the sweat-prints with the hem of her soft jacket, and mouthed an apology.

'To whom am I speaking?' she asked, her voice now an example in cool in the hopes of convincing the man on the other end he hadn't made her blush with a simple *good morning.*

And on a *Monday.* She frowned, clueless as to what *that* could mean.

'Dax,' the voice said. Then, 'Bainbridge,' was added as an afterthought, the dryness of his voice giving her some indication that he was quietly sure she knew exactly who it was.

'Oh, *Da-a-ax.* Hi! How's tricks?'

She slapped a hand over her eyes. That was definitely too chirpy. But that voice of his did things to her so that she forgot all self-control.

From the other side of the Z9 Doug cleared his throat and raised an eyebrow. Caitlyn nodded. Yep, the number-one sexiest thing she'd seen all week was on the phone.

To Dax she said, 'What can I do for you on this fine Monday morning?'

He'd called her on a *Monday.* Maybe he'd left something at her apartment. Or wanted to know the name of a good mechanic. Or—

'You can make my day by telling me that you're free tonight.'

'I'm sorry—pardon?' Caitlyn said.

'Tonight,' he said, more slowly this time. 'Are you free?'

Free? But it had been a one-night stand. Sorbet sex. Hadn't it? 'For what purpose?'

'You want specifics?'

Caitlyn looked around. Doug had shooed off elsewhere leaving her, and the Z9, all on their lonesome. She wriggled her toes to keep the blood from assembling in the one hot spot and said, 'Sure. Why not?'

Through the phone she heard a shuffle and a squeak, and imagined him in a dark suit and tie, up in some lofty city tower, leaning back in a super-comfy leather office chair, looking out of his thousand-storey window, with glorious Melbourne spread out beneath him.

When his voice slid through the phone, deep and slow, the vibrations sent tingles all over her skin.

'I was imagining we'd…' He paused. Long enough she held her breath. Then, '…eat. We could enjoy a little…soft music. No doubt we would…talk. And later, much later, once I've loosened my tie, and you've kicked your shoes off under the table, and we're both nicely pickled in some excellent wine, together we would do…dessert.'

By the time he'd finished she was leaning back hard against the Z9, the cold metal doing nothing to take the edge off her temperature. Somehow she managed to keep her voice from cracking when she said, 'So you're asking me on a date.'

Laughter rolled through the phone. 'I'm asking you to eat dinner with me, but if you'd prefer to call it that—'

'No-o-o!' *Not a date!*

'No?' he repeated after several long beats.

Caitlyn bit her lip. Dax was a man she'd taken home from a bar. For sex. Not as some kind of Hail Mary that it might lead to something more. Her strident rejection of the word 'date' had given her an accidental out if that was what she wanted.

Was it what she wanted?

What she wanted was to see him again. So badly her whole body ached. The want throbbed in time with her pulse—*whoomp, whoomp, whoomp*—from the soles of her feet to the soft depression at the base of her throat.

Other people, people who weren't relationship junkies, did that kind of thing all the time. Had dinner. Had sex. Didn't get engaged to every guy they met. So long as expectations didn't exceed reality, then nobody needed to get hurt.

'Caitlyn?'

'I meant no, I don't need to call it anything.'

'Okay.' His voice slid deep and delicious down the phone. Her shoulders lifted in compensation for the sudden shivers running down her neck.

'I'm working late,' she said, 'so how about we meet up for a drink around nine?' There, a drink. Casual as could be. She named the bar, a fancy hole in the wall she'd glimpsed on occasion down one of Melbourne's many cool quirky alleyways. The kind of place tourists missed, and city-workers flocked to.

'Looking forward to it,' Dax said, and then he was gone.

She took her phone away to find her ear hot and sore from having the phone pressed against it so hard.

'That must have been some phone call.'

Caitlyn jumped, hand slapping against her heart. She turned to find Doug standing about three feet away.

'I've never seen a woman's ankles blush before,' he said.

'My ankles are doing no such thing.'

'If you say so.'

Caitlyn couldn't help it. She glanced at her ankles, bare between her fitted capris and her glossy high-heeled pumps, to find he wasn't kidding. 'Well,' she spluttered, 'then you clearly have a lot to learn about women.'

Doug smiled knowingly back as his eyes slid to the phone she had clasped hard in her sweaty little palm. 'So it seems.'

'Oh, go suck a squeegee.'

Doug's laughter rang through the lofty room while Caitlyn spun away and headed back to the lift before she started laughing too, her high heels all but dancing on the concrete floor.

CHAPTER THREE

Dax sat in a quiet corner of Echoes, nursing a Scotch, and stretching out the rigid muscles of his shoulders. It had been a long and frustrating day. The kind of day that lived down to the very worst of his disillusions. That nobody could be trusted, that life was every man for himself.

He cricked his neck. The only reason he was upright, and not prostrate at the chiropractor, was the five-minute phone call he'd squeezed in to Caitlyn mid-morning. The knowledge that he'd be within touching distance of that soft skin, that silken hair, those warm arms at the end of that day had made the rest tolerable.

A rush of air slid through the bar bringing with it the scent of outdoors. His eyes cut to the door. A posse of twenty-something men in matching grey suits jostled noisily inside.

His fingers clenched harder on the glass, and a muscle in his cheek twitched, as he searched for will power, which was something he usually possessed in spades. His ability to remove himself emotionally from actions and decisions was necessary in the position he held. Stick a soft touch in charge and the foundation's coffers would be empty in a week.

Another rush of air tickled his hair, and his eyes snapped to the door once more. More men, more grey suits.

Will power? What will power? With his skills at compartmentalising, the morning's phone call ought to have been enough to put thoughts of her aside 'til this evening. But it had been something else, something more than just soft skin and silken hair, that had him so gripped with sexual tension if she was another five minutes late the glass was in danger of shattering in his grasp.

The door opened. He felt the breeze, heard the swoosh of traffic, watched the gentle lift of the napkin bedside his glass. He unpeeled his fingers from the now warm glass, one by one; then and only then did he look towards the door.

And there she was, in tight black ankle-skimming pants, a frilled white top and a matching jacket as soft and shimmering as fresh snow. Her hands clutched tight around a tiny beaded purse and her hair was up, soft strands escaping from a low twist. Shafts of silver glinted at her ears. Big eyes the colour of honey scanned the room.

He'd been fully prepared for his memory of her—or more specifically their scorching chemistry—to have been somewhat exaggerated by his euphoric hormones. He'd met her in near darkness, stumbled back to her place in much the same, burned up the bed sheets, and she'd been perfectly content for him to leave while the sun was still warming the other side of the planet. It had been great. Worth repeating. But enough to have him feeling this surge of heat just looking at her?

She licked her lips, and squirmed a little when she couldn't see him, then jutted out a hip in defiance when it appeared to occur to her he might not be there.

Then, just as her mouth began to turn down at the edges, her eyes finally found his: feisty and wholly corrupting. As a secret smile spread to her lips the heat in her eyes softened to a subtle warmth, and it rocketed him right back to how luminous she'd been in his arms.

He hadn't been recalling wrong. She was dazzling. As for their chemistry, she was on the other side of the room, a plethora of blustery city types between them, each trying to suck all the energy from the room, yet his skin contracted as if her fingernails were scraping down his bare chest.

As she walked towards him he felt himself rising off the stool as if some ethereal force were pulling them together.

'Hi,' she said breathily.

His hand moved to her waist as she leant in, the fabric of her jacket giving slightly, turning his mind instantly to soft, warm skin beneath. Her scent wafted past his nose, fresh and sweet, as his lips brushed her proffered cheek. The urge to slide a hand around her small waist and graze his teeth across her neck was consuming.

'So, so sorry I'm late.' Her backside landed on the stool beside his with a thump. 'We're crazy swamped at work at the moment with the launch of the Z9 looming.'

She looked at him as though he ought to be impressed, but he had no idea what she was talking about. 'The Z9?'

'The new production sports model for Pegasus Motors? I work in their PR department and am heading up the big launch in a few months' time, remember?' Her mouth quirked, though her eyes remained locked on his. 'We never quite got to all that, did we?'

'No,' he agreed in a voice so rugged it would have done a pirate proud. 'So I take it the Z9's a car.'

She laughed, tossed her purse onto the bar and motioned to the bartender for a cocktail. 'It's not just "a car". It's a work of art. Poetry in motion. I've seen grown men drool just looking at it, and that's just the engineers who built the thing.'

'Have a picture on you?'

She shook her head. 'Oh, ho, no. You'll have to wait for the big reveal like everyone else.'

Then she snapped her mouth shut and slowly spun on the stool 'til one of her knees slid against one of his. When her eyes grew dark and she puffed out a short sharp breath, he knew she'd felt the same jolt of electricity shoot through her leg that had burned into his.

She said, 'You're mocking me, aren't you?'

'Absolutely.'

'And why?'

'Poetry in motion? It's a *car*.'

One corner of her lovely mouth lifted as her eyes narrowed. 'Were you this cheeky on Saturday? I'm almost certain I wouldn't have taken you home if you were.'

She finished with a shrug, and a small smile, her eyes skimming over him before sliding away. The subsequent roll of her shoulders was akin to saying, *I'm struggling not to picture you naked.* No, not imagine. *Remember.*

And there it was, the thing that had imprinted the hours spent with her deeper onto his mind than usual—her candour.

The way she'd not hidden her attraction to him for a second. The way she'd asked him home simply because she'd wanted to. The way she'd given herself over to him in bed with an abandon he envied. It had all the appearance of being genuine. Even he, the king of the cynics, found himself believing it. Or maybe, that day, he simply wanted to.

He'd spent the morning laying off a guy who'd systematically, over many months, made the foundation's funds his own. A man he'd hired. He'd vetted. He'd respected and liked. And if there was anything still able to chink his well-buffed armour, it was the bitter indignation of being played. If his inept parents had taught him one thing it was that he never wanted to be blindsided like that again.

So having someone look him in the eye and tell it like

it was, was akin to waving a glass of water in front of a man who'd woken up to realise he was alone in the desert.

Gazing at her profile—her slightly dishevelled hair, her thick sooty lashes, her soft pink lips—he took a punt. 'Hungry?'

At the use of her own come-on line from two nights earlier, she blinked. Fast. Her nostrils flared and pink flooded her cheeks. Desire and doubt warring in her ingenuous eyes. But when he smiled her pupils dilated and he could barely see the honey-coloured circle framing them.

Realising it wouldn't take much, he said, 'I know you said drinks, but I missed lunch and could do with a bite.'

Her mouth quirked. 'I was trying to be all cool and nonchalant, if you hadn't noticed.'

'I noticed. You did a commendable job.'

She glanced at the restaurant, and said, 'Sod it. I'm starving. Let's eat.'

'Good. Because I went ahead and reserved a table.'

Her now glinting eyes swung back to him. 'Sure of yourself much?'

'Just enough it would seem. And hungry enough if you'd said no I might have left you here while I ate by myself.'

Her eyebrows shot up a half-second before she burst out laughing. 'Way to make a girl feel special!'

Dax motioned to the maître d', then turned back to her as he said, 'I think we both know I have other ways.'

The pink in her cheeks flooded to her neck, creeping across her collar bone. He ached to feel the heat of her skin, the blood surging so near the surface. He wished he'd never brought up dinner and asked another question instead.

But by then the maître d' was there, and Caitlyn had grabbed her tiny bag and slid off the stool.

He placed his hand in the small of her back and they wove through the growing crowd towards the small table in a low-lit corner of the restaurant, her skin feeling as if it were burning hot against his hand even though the many cruel layers between them meant it was physically impossible.

After five minutes of watching Caitlyn eat her bruschetta, slipping slivers of tomato from the top and sliding them into her mouth, then slowly licking the olive oil from the tips of her finger, Dax knew he needed a new focus or they'd never make it past the entrée. Hell, it wouldn't have mattered to him if they didn't but she'd seemed so excited about dessert.

'So tell me about yourself,' he said, his throat tight.

Caitlyn frowned at him as if he'd said something objectionable, then lifted her shoulders and said, 'What you see is what you get.'

'Really?' He leant forward, enjoying very much the way her breaths hitched every time he did so. 'Then I'm thinking only child. Grew up on a goat farm. Captain of the high-school girls' lacrosse team until you were suspended for ball tampering.'

Her tongue did a sweep of her bottom lip, which made him lose his train of thought, but he picked himself up ably.

'But you went on to complete your schooling in the end, and thank goodness, otherwise you would have missed out on all those lingerie pillow fights with your university roommates.'

Her eyes sparkled deliciously as she licked a stray speck of oregano from her finger. 'You done?'

'My powers of deduction have reached their limits. Though if I missed any of the highlights, or the sordid juicy lowlights for that matter, now's the time to tell me.'

She stilled, her eyes dancing between his, a furrow appearing between her brows. 'You really want to know?'

'You're the one who ordered the soufflé, remember,' he said, sitting back, giving her space. 'We have time to fill.'

When he waited for her to fill the silence, she slowly released her breath, like a balloon losing air through a tiny hole, then said, 'Fine. Only child, yes. Never played lacrosse though. Dancing in front of my bedroom mirror with a hairbrush was about as athletic as I got in high school. And…I grew up on the Central Coast and have never even seen a goat in the flesh.' She frowned at her fingernails. 'My mum lives there still. Same place. Same house. If we didn't have the same knocked knees I'm not sure either of us would believe ourselves related.'

She shook her head, then sat on her hands as if they were the ones she was upset with.

'And your father?' Dax asked, surprising himself at wanting to know when before it had been just conversation.

She gave him a blank stare. 'He didn't have knocked knees.'

His silence stretched again.

She rolled her shoulders, and her eyes for good measure, before saying, 'Mum always said I got my dad's elbows and his nerve. I reckon I look just like him, in fact. He was the complete opposite to her. All spirit and fire. Couldn't stay still even if you sat on him. He travelled constantly. He was a pro rally-car driver actually. A really good one. Did the Dakar rally a few times. He died on the job when I was eleven.'

The speed with which she got out the words and the soft, sad little shrug told him more about her relationship with her dad than even her words had. They'd been close. She missed him still. It was the complete antithesis of the relationship he'd had with his parents, then and now.

'And the pillow fights?' Dax asked, his voice unusually deep.

She slowly looked up at him under her long auburn lashes and the revival of the sparkle in her eyes wiped every other thought from his mind. 'Well, they were way more fun than you could ever imagine. Your turn.'

Dax was still trying to get his head around the image of Caitlyn bouncing about in her underwear, when he heard himself saying, 'Grew up here. Still live here. My parents are both gone.'

Gone. It felt so impersonal. So contrary to the very personal way the event had knocked his values inside out and turned his life upside down.

'I'm sorry to hear that. I—'

'Don't be. It was a long time ago. I have one sister. Younger. Lauren. A semi-reformed hell-raiser. In fact the reason I was at the club the other night was for her birthday. It didn't occur to her that turning thirty might call for something more civilised.'

Caitlyn laughed. 'Why do I get the feeling I'd like her?'

Dax shook his head. 'I'm fairly terrified what might be accomplished if I put the two of you in the same room at the same time.'

'Best not, then,' she said, raising both eyebrows in punctuation, indicating meeting the family was the last thing on her agenda.

'Best not,' he agreed, relaxing back into his chair, thinking he was really going to enjoy her.

'And you run the family business?' she asked.

And just like that Dax's heretofore perfectly content solar plexus tightened as if she'd suddenly brandished a shifting spanner in a threatening manner. His feet pressed into the hardwood floor and his fingers clenched until they felt as if they might never straighten again.

His reaction ought to have been less clamorous, he knew. His position would have come up sooner or later. It always did. His family, their foundation and their fortune were inextricably linked in the public psyche. Along with a widow's peak and a longer second toe, all that came with the Bainbridge name. Only this time he'd apparently been hoping for later.

But after the day he'd had, the battering his usually highly keen self-preservation instincts had taken, it seemed they'd been rehoned to a sharpness that could cut glass.

Caitlyn was a smart girl. She'd clearly noticed his distinct lack of a response. 'My flatmate Franny plus Google means nobody's secrets are safe. She likes to make sure I don't do drinks with wanted axe murderers.'

Dax took a large sip of water. 'Google gave me the thumbs-up?'

'To Franny's satisfaction. Which, in all honesty, isn't saying much.'

Unexpectedly, he laughed, the tension uncurling a tad from his gut. He put the glass down, looked deep into her eyes and saw nothing but genuine interest. In what he did, sure. In who he was, certainly. But mostly in him. The lick of desire from the other night hadn't waned. It was there for all the world to see.

'I am the CEO of the Bainbridge Foundation,' he acknowledged.

'So Google said. What does that entail exactly?' Elbow on the table, she cupped her chin in her upturned palm and slid another piece of oil-soaked bread into her mouth.

His eyes remained glued there as he said, 'Primarily I keep track of the investment side of the foundation's funds. Finance was my career before… Before I took over.'

She crossed her eyes at him. 'Investments are a mystery to me. If the stock market isn't just a way for clever sorts to create money out of nothing then I don't know what it is.'

Another smile swept across his face, surprising him

again. 'I like it because it's clean. It follows patterns if you know how to read them. If you pay attention it won't surprise you. If only you could take out the human factor it would be perfect.'

'You like numbers more than people?'

'Numbers are predictable. Constant. People, in my experience, are mostly neither.'

'Funny,' she said, 'that's what I like most about people. Every person you meet has the potential of making for an exciting new adventure.'

She slowly licked a stray tomato seed from her pointer finger, and his eyes snagged on her mouth, and bit by bit he felt the tension in his gut ease completely away. It had to if he wanted to make room for the far more enjoyable sensation brought on by watching her teeth scrape over her nail.

She clicked her fingers at him and he flinched. 'So that's why you have a private number! When you called this morning and no number came up, my first thought was that you were a telemarketer. Lucky for you I was distracted enough to answer anyway.'

'Lucky for me.' Her eyes locked onto his and he could feel something pure and physical tug between them.

'But what if I wanted to contact you?' she asked.

'You'd have to call the foundation and leave a message with my assistant's assistant.'

'Your assistant's assistant? Wow. You're cut-throat.'

'You have no idea.'

The waiter arrived with their entrées, a pile of gorgeous, glistening prawns lathered in deliciously pungent garlic.

When the kid left Dax looked over to find Caitlyn watching him, her fork turning over and over between her fingers, a small smile on her face making him think she was trying to figure him out.

Until she said, 'You really didn't Google me before calling me this morning?'

He shook his head.

'Pity,' she said, piercing a prawn with one hard hit. 'Look hard enough and there are pictures that'd make your toes curl.'

An hour later, their dessert plates were mere crumbs. Dax had downed his espresso in one hit, and his feet now tapped on the floor, ready to spring into action the second she gave the sign she was ready.

Having been forced to watch her hum happily over every bite of her steak and lick the spoon clean with every mouthful of dessert, his body felt so tight with desire he had to grit his teeth to bite it back.

And now, considering the look in Caitlyn's eyes as she gazed hungrily at the mint balancing on the edge of his saucer, Dax had never felt so envious of a food in his life.

'Want it?' he asked, reverting to monosyllables.

She glanced up, guilty at having been caught. 'What? That? No. I couldn't possibly fit another…' Her eyes slunk back to his saucer. 'Oh, just give it to me, will you?'

He slid his cup to her side of the table. She all but bounced on her seat as she slowly turned the saucer around, then placed the wafer-thin chocolate on the tip of a finger, brought it up to eye level, seemed to say a small prayer of thanks, then closed her eyes and tipped it onto her tongue.

As if it had finally snapped its leash his mind ran wild. Her place? His? Which was closer? Was her flatmate home? She had a flatmate, right? His place, then. Was his bed made? Who cared? The way his blood was cooking they'd be lucky to get to the bed.

'Done?' he asked, the caveman deep inside him now very much in charge.

She flicked her fringe from her face, licked a smidge of chocolate from her lip and looked him in the eye. She sat back, folded her hands on the table, and at the determined look in her eye his libido actually whimpered.

'Before… Before we finish up, I have a confession to make,' she announced.

Damn it! Why now? Why that? They'd been so close!

He considered deflecting her—'til later, 'til after—but knew himself too well to know she'd tweaked his Achilles' heel, and the ignorance would play with his head worse than the knowing.

'Go on, then,' he said. 'Hit me.'

'Okay. Here goes.' She screwed her eyes shut and held her breath and said, 'I was on a date the night we met. With another guy.'

A date. A *date*? The concept bounced about inside his head, making no sense. She hadn't stalked him. Or secretly pricked a hole in his condom. Or used truth serum to finagle the company's banking passwords from his mind. Bloody hell, had he become so accustomed to believing people were always out for themselves that he'd really considered any of those options seriously?

What mattered was that he'd been thrown a bone, a bright ray of honesty where he'd expected cunning, and he'd be a cold-hearted bastard if he didn't take it. Dax laughed 'til his stomach hurt.

'That was really embarrassing to admit, and now you're laughing at me!' She glared at him accusingly, as if he were the one who'd done something improper.

'What did you expect me to do?'

'I'm not sure. Cast me off in the name of brotherhood.'

He motioned to a passing waiter for the bill, waving his credit card. 'Do I know the guy? Is he a direct relative?'

'I'm not sure. Franny didn't Google that deep. Are you related to anyone who sells surfboards in Torquay?'

He slanted her a sideways look.

Her smile was seductive as all hell as she shrugged unapologetically. 'Believe me, that was a selling point.'

Dax ignored the hot stab of jealousy and said, 'In case you haven't noticed, I am a Man. The concept of besting another Man at something is a happy one. You chose me. I won. Tonight my manhood reigns supreme.'

When she laughed her cheeks grew pink and her eyes sparkled. 'You're shameful!'

'I'm not the one who ditched a date for a one-night stand.'

His hand edged across the table until his little finger found hers. Her voice was husky as she said, 'So you do think I'm a hussy.'

'Absolutely. And for that I will be eternally grateful.'

Banter on the backburner, searing heat arced between them. She sat very still, but her gorgeous eyes drank him in. They were the colour of good Scotch. Of autumn leaves. Hell, she was making him a poet.

'Dax…' she said, then stopped.

'More confessions?' he asked, past the point of caring if there were.

A smile came and went. 'More like fine print. I'm… I'm not looking for anything serious right now.'

He stilled, surprised to say the least, until he realised it wasn't a brush-off. It was providence. He wanted her. God, did he want her. But only to a point. He didn't do commitment, which mostly came down to a complete lack of faith that anything that seemed genuine really was. He'd been proven right on that score too many times to change his mind. He barely trusted his housekeeper with a key—much less a 'girlfriend'—and he'd known her for fifteen years. And that wasn't easily put into words without offending.

Dax said, 'Is now an appropriate time for me to message my mates and tell them I've found the perfect woman, or would that be presumptuous?'

'Go ahead,' she said, leaning back in the chair, a secret smile playing on her lips. 'I don't have anywhere else to be.'

'Oh, but I think you do.' Not taking his eyes off her, he pushed back his chair and made it around to her side of the table in time to slide hers away.

She glanced up at him in thanks. And again as he held out her jacket.

'How far is your car?' he asked once they were making their way, fast, through the still-busy bar.

'I caught a cab.'

By now he could feel his pulse beating all the way to his toes. 'So were you hoping we'd only need one car between us by this point, or were you planning on getting sloshed? I'm not sure either has helped in your efforts to clean up your image.'

She glanced back over her shoulder, gleaming brown eyes, shining auburn hair, glints of light catching on metallic threads in her jacket. She lit up the room. 'Where your mind goes reflects far more on you, my friend, than it does on me. I get a car as part of my work agreement and I'm between freebies right now.'

'Convenient.'

She laughed. Heads turned. All male. Dax felt himself strut.

He closed in on her, placing a hand in the small of her back. She started at the touch, then sank into it. Into *him*.

His voice was tight, hell, his whole body felt like a coiled spring as he said, 'Then please allow me to escort you home. Casually, of course.'

She raised a silky eyebrow. 'Casually? How does that work? Will you be driving with your elbow on the open window sill, easy-listening radio humming through the speakers?'

'And I thought you were the one who liked new adventures.'

She laughed, the sound tense, fluttery, excited. 'If it's not out of your way—'

'It's not.' It was closer than his place, which was all that mattered.

Once outside, the crispness of the spring evening air came as a shock when compared with the heat that had been bubbling between then all night.

'Come here,' he said. And he didn't have to ask twice.

She turned to him, slid her arms beneath his jacket, around his waist, the friction of her soft hands on the cotton of his shirt almost painful. She pressed herself against him and the trembling in her body told him he wasn't alone in the need to get skin to skin as fast as humanly possible.

The revving of an engine cut into his thoughts. A familiar engine, thank God. He gave her a little shove towards the car, knowing if he didn't do it then he might never get the strength to let her go at all.

'You have a driver?' She leant down to wave through the tinted windows, her pants pulling tight across her backside.

Dax cut his eyes to the clear cloudless sky and prayed for strength. 'If I have to get to the airport it's easier than driving myself.'

'The airport?'

'I was in a meeting in Sydney all day today.'

She stood up, blinking at him. 'Why didn't you stay overnight?'

'I had plans.'

'Oh? *Oh.*' The heat that shone from her gorgeous amber eyes was worth every second of the weary flight back.

He opened the car door.

She shuffled in and leant across the partition, hand outstretched. 'Caitlyn March,' she said.

'Jerry Weidman.'

She sat back, ran her hands over the leather seat. 'Nice wheels, Jerry.'

'Thank you, Ms March. Now where can I take you on this fine evening?'

Caitlyn barely paused before giving her address, and then Jerry, bless him, slid the privacy screen into place before doing a smooth U-turn and taking off down the gleaming Melbourne street.

'Nice wheels?' Dax murmured, his voice echoing in the dark confined space.

'They are,' she said, slanting her eyes his way. 'I should know.'

Wisps of her fringe had fallen from her hairdo and now tickled the edge of her cheek. He reached out and tucked it behind her ear. The blaze of attraction flared in her eyes, creating hot dark pools of desire in their whisky-brown depths.

Sliding his hand around her neck, he leaned over, kissing her gently. Intending to mark his place, to light the spark that would flame long into the night if he had any say in the matter. But when she opened her mouth and slid her hands into his hair, he was on top of her in a red-hot second.

Such soft hair, soft lips, soft curves, soft moans.

Her legs wrapped about him, pulling him close, making him curse his clothes and hers. Making him want to give Jerry a bonus for not sending them sprawling into the leg space each time he turned a brilliantly smooth corner.

All too soon the car pulled to a halt. Dax looked up,

frowning, to discover they'd pulled up in front of a neat, sprawling, rendered apartment building.

He looked back at Caitlyn, who was watching him, eyes heavy with desire, a self-satisfied smile warming her face, more silky auburn strands tumbling from her hair. Never in his life had he met a woman who looked so delicious when dishevelled.

Jerry, pro that he was, refrained from opening the car door for them, leaving Dax to do the honours as he and Caitlyn tumbled on less than able legs onto the pavement. Jerry then pulled away discreetly and found a park down the block, leaving Dax to walk behind Caitlyn as she sashayed through her front gate and inside the building.

Somehow they managed to keep their hands off one another in the short lift ride to her floor. Having her so close and not touching her only turned the heat up more.

At her apartment door she said, 'Franny, my flatmate, isn't home.'

'No?' Dax asked, fighting back a smile.

'She's a flight attendant. Away a lot.'

'I like her already,' Dax said, after which he tumbled Caitlyn inside, kissing away anything else either of them possibly wanted to say.

Much later, when the world was still dark, and the first birds heralded the coming of the sun, Dax woke Caitlyn with a kiss. She slid a hand into his hair as she kissed him back.

'Caitlyn,' he said, his voice hoarse with the need to leave and not to disentangle her warm naked body from her sheets.

'Mmm?'

'Where's your mobile?'

She waved a hand towards her night stand. He found

her phone—white with red butterflies dancing across the back— figured out the menu, jabbed in several numbers and placed it in her open hand. Propped up on an elbow now, lids heavy with sleep, she slowly realised what he'd done.

'Is that *your* number?' she asked, sitting up higher so that the sheet slid from her back, revealing the top of her perfect creamy bottom. 'Your special secret bat-phone number?'

He dragged his eyes back to her face. 'I didn't want you mistaking me for a telemarketer and not answering when I call.'

The hesitant smile that hovered on her face gave him the strangest feeling in the pit of his stomach.

'And I will call,' he added. 'Casually, of course.'

She shook her hair from her face, and gave a good impression of nonchalance. If only she didn't look so well tumbled she might have pulled it off. 'I can't stop you calling. But at least this way if I don't answer you'll know it's because I don't want to talk to you.'

He felt himself grinning.

She lifted her phone, pointed it at him, then the click of the camera function split the quiet air. Her eyes slid from the phone back to him, her cheeks blushing pink. In that moment she seemed so soft and vulnerable he had to curl his fingernails into the pads of his palm so as not to wrap his hands about her face and kiss her until morning.

It was enough to have him taking a determined step back. Then with a sharp salute he walked away.

For now.

CHAPTER FOUR

'I've barely seen you the last couple of weeks,' Franny said as together she and Caitlyn collected yoga mats, blankets, straps, and blocks from the box at the back of the Hawthorn Hatha Yoga studio. 'Whatcha been up to?'

'Work, you know.' Caitlyn scoped out a spot near the back and slightly behind someone so the yoga instructor wouldn't pick up on her wandering lunges again.

'All work? No play?'

Caitlyn slid a glance sideways, then concentrated on unfurling her yoga mat. 'Some play.'

'I knew it! You and Dax are so a thing, aren't you?'

'God, no! Not in the least. In fact we've been very grown up about it all and agreed that we're going to be totally casual. In fact since dinner last week we've had lunch once.'

Lunch being a bowl of chocolate-covered strawberries in bed as delivered by room service of a gorgeous boutique hotel exactly halfway between Dax's office and hers. Just thinking about it made her knees quiver more than even the hardest yoga standing postures did.

'On your backs,' the instructor called out as soothingly as she could in a room the size of a basketball court. The lights were dimmed and relaxing eastern music played over the speakers. 'Eyes closed. Clear your minds.'

'On your back, eyes closed, dim lights,' Franny whispered. 'Sounds like anyone you know?'

Caitlyn threw a sock at her.

After snoring loudly through the breathing practice, Franny perked up when they began their floor postures. 'Please tell me there has been lots and lots of athletic lovemaking.'

'I'm telling you no such thing,' Caitlyn said on an outward breath as she touched her toes to the floor over her head.

'Turn on your core!' the instructor called out.

Caitlyn did as she was told, or as close as possible when not exactly certain where her core was.

'Then tell me this,' Franny said. 'Is the gelato sex working?'

'*Sorbet* sex. And yeah, crazily enough, I think it is.'

She realised then, with a stab of something that felt a lot like guilt, that she'd barely thought about George, or any of her other dud relationships, in days.

But no wonder. It was as though Dax had imprinted himself on her as no other man had. Even when she wasn't with him, she could feel him as if it had been mere minutes rather than days since they'd last touched. As if her muscle memory were permanently primed, just waiting for the moment it could give into him once again. In the face of all that heat, there was simply no room for depressing thought.

'So you're really not an item?'

'We're really not.' If she'd needed any proof of that it had been how hard finding time to get together had been. She was used to being pursued, but Dax's schedule—and greater self-control than hers—made it hard to pin him down. He hadn't come running at every crook of her finger, which was new. New, and actually kind of provocative.

'And you're honestly okay with that?'

'Honestly I am. I'm thrilled. It's so liberating. The pressure's off. I can just have fun. And he's perfectly happy to keep things casual too.'

Franny snorted. 'Well, of course he is. He's a man. He probably thinks he's found the Holy Grail.'

'Maybe we both have.'

While Franny mmmmed and pffted, clearly not so convinced, Caitlyn closed her eyes and pretended to be thinking about her breathing and nothing else, when really she was thinking so specifically of something else she could literally taste chocolate-covered strawberries. And soon she began to ache for Dax in a way that even the deepest yogic meditation wasn't going to fix.

'Now on your knees and into extended child pose,' the instructor called. 'Lengthen your spine on the in breath; push your chest forward on the out breath.'

Head on the floor, arms stretched over her head, Caitlyn glanced through the gap underneath her underarm and stage-whispered, 'I'm seeing him this weekend and I'm telling you now there'll be more casual athletic sorbet sex than even you can imagine.'

Franny peeked from beneath her underarm and grinned. 'That's my girl.'

She wasn't, in fact, seeing Dax that weekend. Not officially. Not yet. But the apartment was all hers that weekend as Franny had a layover in Perth and she thought it was about time to send him links to the pictures he hadn't bothered to Google. Bikinis and coconut oil were involved and she'd had a horrible stomach flu that summer and had never looked better.

A thrill skittered through her at the thought of having his hands on her again so soon. Not soon enough. It filled her 'til she felt tight from the top of her thighs to her belly button, 'til she could fill her lungs so far as her upper chest.

Ah! she thought suddenly, holding her position. *So that's what turning on my core feels like!*

Who needed yoga when you had Dax Bainbridge?

It had been one hell of a week.

Rumours of more embezzlement within the foundation were beginning to get a grip. With over five hundred employees around the world, it was going to take an investigation and a half to even hope to smoke the culprits out.

If Dax had made plans to be any other place, he would have cancelled in a heartbeat, instead chaining himself to his desk another night if that was what it took to yank the company back to submission.

Hell, if he were any other man he'd probably have limped home, kicked off his shoes, grabbed himself a cold beer, and fallen asleep on the couch in front of the footy.

But he was who he was, and as such believed his responsibilities to his sister, his employees, the shareholders, to restoring the family name were too great. That might have daunted another man. He merely broadened his shoulders and got on with things.

But for whatever reason, maybe the extra pressure of the week, or maybe the destination itself, he'd decided to give himself a rare break.

He stood at Caitlyn's security gate, his eyes grazing the brickwork until he found the warm light of her window. No dinner plans. No drinks first. No stolen half-hour and rush back to work. Just her. And an empty apartment.

He buzzed the bell with purpose in his finger.

'Dax? You're early! Or am I late?' her bright voice hummed through the speaker.

Despite himself he smiled. 'Would you prefer I take a lap around the block?'

Her answer came in the buzzing sound that heralded the unlocking of the gate.

When he finally knocked on her apartment door, it took a few seconds before it opened with a flourish.

'You're definitely early,' Caitlyn said again, pressing a hand to one pink cheek. Her voice was breathy. Her auburn hair tied in a loose knot atop her head. Her jeans tight. Her top soft and loose. White powder streaked across her other cheek. Her feet were bare bar pale pink polish, which twinkled up at him.

She looked so fresh, so wholesome, desire coiled deep through his middle, and the only word that spun from the thick foggy swirl of his sub-conscious to mind was a long, slow, *Da-a-amn*.

'Everything okay?' she asked, brow furrowed.

He nodded, speechless, Cro-Magnon Man incarnate. At the rise of his caveman instincts all he wanted to do was touch her, to hold her, to allow her natural warmth to wash away the detritus of his week. He moved to take her. The couch looked comfortable enough, even if a little small—

A loud beeping echoed through the apartment.

Then Caitlyn was off, disappearing through a pair of white-panelled saloon doors into a room he assumed was the kitchen.

He took a step inside, squinting against the late spring sunshine streaming through the gauzy curtains onto the pale yellow walls and cosy furniture. Rugs you could slide your toes through. Couches so soft you'd sink into them and struggle to get back out. A floral padded window seat was covered in a haphazard array of magazines. A vase of daisies that had seen better days sat askew on a sideboard above which rested a mirror that boasted photos of Caitlyn and friends poking haphazardly out of its frame.

The place was charming and warm. Her. As he'd un-
consciously known he would, he slowly felt himself relax.

'I'm sorry I'm running so late,' her disembodied voice
called from the other room. 'I forgot I had to make cup-
cakes!'

'For dinner?'

'Alas no. One of the guys at work's wife had a baby last
week and it's his toddler's birthday this week so I'm helping a tiny bit.'

He shucked off his jacket and tie, laying them over the
back of a dining chair.

She poked her head over the saloon doors. Strands of
straight auburn hair fell down her cheeks. 'Want a glass of
wine while you wait?'

'Thanks,' he managed. Though awareness of what he
was waiting *for* tightened his throat 'til he could barely
swallow.

A minute later she pushed the doors open with her backside and padded into the lounge. They said high heels did
things to a woman's hips as they walked. But watching
Caitlyn pad across the carpet in bare feet, two generous
glasses of red in her hands, he wasn't sure he'd ever seen
anything sexier.

She slid a foot to her calf as she leant against the back
of a couch. Then in silence, they watched one another over
their untouched glasses of wine. The heat from the kitchen
had nothing on the way they built the temperature in that
room all on their own.

He wondered exactly when his need to grow the family
business had become such an inordinate obsession that he
let it keep him from this, from her, from indulging in such
a basic human need, when it was there for the taking. There
had been moments, more than he could count, when he'd
felt less than amorous towards the work he did, but in that

moment, with all that lusciousness within such easy reach, he cursed it with a passion he hadn't known he possessed.

She hitched the strap of her top, which had done a kamikaze over her shoulder, giving him a peekaboo glimpse of a dark pink bra strap, then said, 'I had planned to answer the door looking way more glamorous. And wearing sexy underthings. So drink up, and give me two minutes to change. I'll be a new woman.'

The thing was he didn't want a new woman. He wanted this one, every warm, sweet, honest bit of her, and he wasn't willing to wait a minute longer, much less two.

He took her wine glass from her hand and placed it, along with his, on the closest horizontal surface, and then he wrapped a hand around her wrist and pulled her to him with a tug. Her breath hitched as she tumbled against him, her fingers gripping his shirt, one of her knees sliding between his.

'You're not into sexy underthings?' she asked, her voice husky with the same desire that swirled hot and deep in her molten honey eyes.

'Not nearly so much as I'm interested in what you keep hidden beneath them.'

His eyes slid to her mouth where a tiny speck of pale pink icing rested in the corner. Her tongue shot out to lick it away. She got it all. He pretended otherwise, reaching out his thumb to stroke her lip, bewitched by the pull of soft skin against the rough of his thumb pad. He then lifted his thumb and sucked the end, imagining the taste of her on his tongue.

'But they're really nice underthings. With lacy bits, and see-through bits, and bits that come apart just by looking at them,' she said, her voice thick. 'I promise. Two minutes.'

'I've waited long enough.'

With that he kissed her. The pent-up frustration that had

built up within him after so much time without her touch, her taste, her warmth, spilt over until his need for her was no longer within his control.

She whimpered as she kissed him back, her hands digging into his hair, her hips pressing into him, her back arching as she all but tried to climb inside him.

When they'd kissed 'til he could barely feel his mouth any more, he pulled away. Her lips were pink and swollen, her eyes dark and drunk with desire. Without another word he swept her into his arms and carried her into her bedroom.

Then his hands were at her hips, his mouth on hers. He'd never in his life tasted anything so sweet. Like sugar and berries and cream. He was sure he hadn't eaten a cupcake since he was in primary school, but he knew he'd be rectifying that miserable truth as soon as humanly possible. But for now he had another conquest in mind.

Caitlyn's hands were tugging, tearing at his shirt. Hating to leave those lips alone for any longer than necessary, he yanked it over his head and threw it to the floor and was back to kissing her again.

She lifted her arms, so loose and lazy they might as well have been boneless, as he slid her diaphanous top away without impediment.

They kissed like teenagers who'd just figured out how it was really done and saw no reason not to kiss like that for ever. Deep, wet, lush kisses that turned his brain to pulp.

Then the rest of his body began to make itself known. To demand to be a part of the seduction. And in ways his teenaged self hadn't even dreamt of.

He pressed her back onto her bed, smoothly pinning her arms above her head. With his eyes he told her she wasn't to move. The smile that bloomed at the corner of her mouth told him she was perfectly happy to do as she was told.

She clung to the bedding, to the wrought-iron bed head, to him as she writhed blissfully beneath him as he made sure not one inch of her glorious body was left unadored.

Her complete fearlessness made the entire experience exquisite. And as she came, again and again beneath his touch, her eyes clung to him, searing, stunned, leaving him feeling so strong in the face of the fragility he could bring out in her.

Then, with trembling fingers, she put her hands to his cheeks and wrapped her legs about his hips. She drew him inside her; achingly slow, achingly deep.

They said not a word. In fact they hadn't said a single thing to one another since he'd first taken her hand. Yet he knew everything she was thinking, everything she was feeling, simply by looking into her eyes as he rocked above her.

Pressure built on such waves of painful pleasure he just held on tight and rode them to their powerful crest. As he came he felt relief. Release. His muscles were loose. His nerves near numb. His mind a void. As he lay in her arms, breathing heavily, his slick hot limbs intertwined with hers, he had the vaguest sense that his mind was usually filled with concerns, anxieties, duties, only now there was nothing but a warm hum.

The only thought that filtered into the void in his head, floating like a thin silver ribbon in gentle free fall, was if ever there was a week when he'd most needed to find a woman who brought him no extra stress, and who explicitly wanted a no-strings fling, this was it.

Karma had finally decided to pay up.

Caitlyn lay curled up on her bed, her breaths finally returning to something akin to normal.

Dax's arm lay heavily across her waist as his breaths

took on the even deep rhythm of a man asleep. While her mind spun a million times a minute.

What they'd experienced hadn't been so much the fun, frolicsome, yogic athleticism she'd promised Franny. Neither had it been the hot lusty sex they'd experienced before.

This had been deeply sensual.

Her bones felt like warm butter. She was acutely aware that the skin from her toes to her scalp was all one piece as it hummed the same note. Her blood throbbed so powerfully, so deeply, it was as if it had found the pulse of the earth. Emotion still ran so high within her every now and then she had to fight back tears of relief that were stinging the backs of her eyes.

That hadn't felt like simple sex with a semi-stranger. She'd looked into him, let him see into her. It had felt like making love.

'It wasn't,' she whispered aloud, biting her tongue when Dax moved slowly behind her, his big body folding itself divinely around hers.

It was just sex, she told herself silently this time. It was just that he was so very very good at it. Or maybe they were simply very very good at it together.

In an effort to make sure, she was forced to do exactly what she'd been trying to avoid doing—she thought about her past boyfriends. She had to in order to make sure Dax was different, and that the very fact that their chemistry was so awesome was a good thing, and not a portent of impending doom.

The guys she dated were usually *nice* guys. Sweet and uncomplicated. Like human Labradors. The kind of men who poured affection on a girl as soon as looking at them. The kind of affection she always mistook for true love.

Dax on the other hand was razor-sharp. She wondered

if he was even a little restless. Sometimes it felt like being with her gave him an out for a while. That made him complicated enough it'd take a lifetime to unravel him.

She ran a gentle finger down his arm, over the long thick veins straining near the surface, through the light spray of dark hair, over the large bones of his wrist, and across fingers that could make a woman's body feel as if it were being turned inside out.

Maybe that was her biggest safety net of all, that he was too much for her. Looking up at him always made her breathless, as if she were breathing rarefied air. And he had this kind of restrained power pulsing just beneath his skin, the kind that often made her feel small. Delicate even. Not herself at all.

Dax Bainbridge was too complicated, too strong, too beautiful. Too much.

She breathed in deep, and breathed out comforted. With all that going on she was in absolutely no danger of falling into the same old trap of thinking herself in love with him.

CHAPTER FIVE

'ANOTHER, and make it a double!' Franny demanded of Ivan the bartender after her date had kissed her on the back of the hand and excused himself to 'freshen up'.

Caitlyn sat next to Franny on their usual barstools at the Sand Bar, trying to keep a straight face, but in the end she cracked up laughing. 'Where on earth did you find *that* guy?'

Franny crumpled until her face landed in her palms. 'Mymothersetmeup.'

'I'm sorry, did you just say your mother set you up?'

'He's her hairdresser's son. She promised me Jace was tall, had a job, and his own apartment—'

'Clearly we should book the wedding chapel immediately!'

Franny sobbed. 'Why me?'

'Because you're not in the least bit picky.'

Franny sat up and glared. 'At least mine turned up. Where's yours?'

Caitlyn opened her mouth, then snapped it shut. Franny knew how to push her buttons, that much was sure. She'd played her good, mooching about the apartment because Caitlyn had stumbled on the perfect non-relationship— poor Franny couldn't even manage that, so please please please could they double date just this once?

When Franny disappeared into her cocktail Caitlyn glanced discreetly at her watch, then her phone, then towards the door, her towering black satin heels slapping restlessly against the soles of her feet.

If Dax didn't turn up, she couldn't blame him. The second she'd opened her mouth to ask, she'd known it was blurring the edges of what they were doing. But then after a painfully long pause, he'd agreed, only if she promised to make it worth his while. As if that were any kind of punishment!

But the truth was, a couple of times when they'd hooked up in the past few weeks she'd found herself feeling things. Delicious addictive things. Things she ought not to have been feeling, for damn sure. She'd partly gone through with Franny's plea because the thought of having a chaperone or two for a night felt like a good thing.

The music shifted tone. Loud thumping beats reverberated through her body. She squirmed on her stool, tugging tastefully at her lacy black cocktail dress with the deceptively demure shoulder frills that only brought the attention to the not-so-demure neckline.

She was wearing new lingerie. She'd seen them in a shop window on the way to work and thought of Dax. Of Dax taking them off with his teeth to be more precise. She'd bought the set without even looking at the price tag.

They were frilly and peach-coloured and soft as baby's breath. And just a little itchy to tell the truth. Or maybe that was just her body's reaction to the knowledge Dax would be there soon, his warm hand finding any excuse to touch her, his delicious scent wrapping itself tight around her, her nerves jangling every time she caught his dark gaze drifting over her bare skin.

Just then something in the bar changed, the atmosphere around her shifted, thickened and she spun on the stool to find Dax walking towards her. In place of his usual suit and tie he wore dark jeans, a chocolaty linen jacket, and a cream V-neck sweater. He was unshaven. His dark hair a little spikier than usual.

To the untrained eye he might have appeared perfectly casual, perfectly appropriate for the venue. To Caitlyn— whose heart leapt into her throat—he looked positively dangerous.

His eyes found hers, the dark hazel depths glinting. A hint of a smile tugged at the corner of his mouth. The music was drowned out by the sudden rush of blood in her ears. And as his eyes took in her dress, her formidable shoes, the daring V at her décolletage, the smile deepened in appreciation and she felt herself go over all faint.

So much for the safety of numbers. She had the feeling if he had the inclination to sweep the drinks and pretzels from the bar so that he might take her then and there she wouldn't have it in her to stop him.

Thankfully he had more restraint. When he approached he leaned down and kissed her. On the mouth. A long, slow, deliberate kiss that showed the world—or at least those inside the bar who happened to be looking their way—that the dress and shoes were for his benefit, not theirs.

Then the kiss lingered. Deepened. She felt all resolve begin to dissolve. Oh, God!

She pressed her hand into his chest and pulled away, breathless and slightly shaken. A muscle twitched in his jaw as his hot dark eyes burned into hers.

A hand jabbed in between them, reminding them both they weren't alone.

'Hiya! I'm Franny. You must be Caitlyn's guy.'

Her guy? Caitlyn turned just enough to glare at her. 'Franny, this is my *friend* Dax Bainbridge. Dax, Franny Anderson.'

She noticed a slight cooling in Dax as he took Franny's hand. Not aloofness as such, just a cessation of heat. Heat that was meant for her alone. She bit back the unexpected smile that she felt blooming right down in her stomach.

'Frances?' Dax asked.

Caitlyn watched in no surprise as Franny melted under his attention. 'Francesca.'

'Lovely. A pleasure to finally meet you, Francesca.'

Franny blushed, and giggled, and finished off with a hiccup. Caitlyn had to give her friend a bump so that she'd let go of Dax's hand.

He said, 'I was led to believe there would be a fourth.' Dax moved nearer, and Caitlyn clenched her buttocks on the stool so as not to sway towards him. Until his hand slid to her lower back, branding her with its heat, reminding her the price she was yet to pay.

'Hmm?' Franny hummed.

'Jace,' Caitlyn reminded her. '*Your* date.'

Franny's memory returned with all the subtlety of a bucket of iced water over her head. She shuddered, sucked down the rest of her cocktail, motioned frantically to Ivan behind the bar for another, then with her lip curled said, 'He's off somewhere reapplying his lipstick.'

Dax managed to keep a straight face while turning to Caitlyn, a subtle question in his eyes.

She said, 'You'll understand soon enough.'

'I can't wait.'

Dax's eyes narrowed, and focused, and Caitlyn knew without any doubt that which he couldn't wait for had nothing to do with Franny or her date. She had to cross her legs so as to contain the fire lighting her up from the inside.

Later, after a strange and memorable dinner, as the menfolk sat at their corner table talking baseball, or football, or balls of some kind, Caitlyn and Franny took the opportunity to sit at the bar and compare notes.

'You are a stronger woman than I,' Franny said with a sigh. 'I wouldn't have the hide to call sleeping with *that* gelato sex—'

'Sorbet.'

'Right. But sorbet's so cold, and he's just so big and yummy and intense. I'd call it…flambé sex!'

Caitlyn's gaze wandered over to Dax. She sucked the cherry from her cocktail stick and let it slide around the inside of her mouth.

Franny's voice sounded as if it were coming from a long way away when she said, 'It's like you are flambéing away all thoughts of old flames, yes?'

'Uh-huh.'

'Now, that didn't sound as vehement as I would have liked. What's going on?'

'It's fine. Great even. Flambé central. Only… Only I've had a few moments when I've felt myself slipping. Just a little. Franny, my will power just sucks.'

The truth was she'd never been that good at denying herself, a definite leftover from her dad. Her mum could go months without calling after one of their many 'differences of opinion', her will power was that exceptional, whereas her dad had been impossible to pin down. He'd tried staying home but in the end the call of adventure was always greater. In the end it had killed him.

Falling for every guy she met wasn't going to kill her. But emotionally? It was like a slow, unpleasant haemorrhaging of her heart, and of late she'd become frightened that one day she'd wake up to find there was simply nothing left.

'Rubbish,' Franny shot back. '*I* have no will power. You can look at a glass display filled with cakes and choose the apple strudel. I will always, and I mean *always*, pick the double devil chocolate mud cake, no matter how much I know it's bad for me.'

Caitlyn frowned, paying close attention to the jittery feeling watching Dax created inside her. 'Maybe. But when it comes to men... That's where I always fall down.'

Franny's silence was a sign of her tacit agreement.

Caitlyn said, 'I try to be good. I really do. But when a guy gets that look in his eye—'

'I know the look you mean. Like it's taking every ounce of will power *he* has not to gobble you up.'

'No. Not that. When a man looks at me like he can't believe that of all the men in the world I picked him...' Caitlyn's shoulders rounded as a familiar liquid warmth shot through her. 'I just can't resist.'

Franny cleared her throat. 'Honey, that's not will power. Will power is being confronted with the "gobble you up" look and managing to keep your undies on. As for that other look? That's being in love with the idea of being in love.'

'No. No! No?'

'Think about it. When you have to say no you *can*. How many relationships have you ended? Not just the engagements, but even before you started taking things to such extremes? You have will power. You only seem to wield it when you have no other choice.'

With three cocktails and a pretty meagre plate of barbecue calamari taking the edge off, Caitlyn's defences were pretty tenuous and she let all that sink in. Franny had made a fair point. Maybe even two. She did have the will power to do the right thing, she only needed to learn how to exercise it more sensibly.

Breaking into her big epiphany, Franny said, 'The big question is, is Dax double devil chocolate mud cake or is he apple strudel?'

Caitlyn quietly thought that the big question was, with her history, would it make any difference?

'Either way I like him,' Franny said decidedly. 'Don't panic. You can have him.'

Caitlyn laughed, rather glad the subject had been changed. 'Can I now?'

Franny nodded. 'I prefer my men more...'

'Dumb?'

'I was going to say happy-go-lucky, but okay. Brawn over brain suits me just fine.'

Caitlyn kept her next thought to herself. The knowledge that Dax had it all. Brawn, brain, wit, and more sex appeal than a room full of firemen.

As if he'd been summoned by her very thoughts, Dax's warm hand landed on her waist. Her breath hitched in her throat as he spun her around and into a solid wall of male chest. Her hands curled around a pair of cool jacket lapels, reminding her vividly of the first time they'd met.

'Dance with me,' Dax said, and it wasn't a question.

Franny's envious sigh barely registered in the periphery of Caitlyn's consciousness.

Franny said, 'Dance with the man, for Pete's sake. I'd better go track down my very confused date.'

Two slow songs in Caitlyn felt so loose and warm she leant her head on Dax's chest, enjoying the unfamiliar feeling of a man who could lead. He had such grace and timing it was easy. Natural. Sexy as hell.

She snuck her hand from his shoulder into the hair at the back of his neck, loving the feel of all that velvety softness raking against her sensitive fingertips.

Dax's hand slid down onto her hip, pressing her so close that every bit of her body that could found a companion in every bit of him.

It occurred to her for a brief moment that anyone watching would have no doubt they were in the midst of a particularly sensual and very public bout of foreplay. Right on top of that it occurred to her that she simply didn't care.

It felt too good. *He* felt too good.

Whatever they were to one another—sorbet or flambé—when she was in his arms all she knew was that it didn't feel the same as before. There was none of the panicked impatience to get things moving faster, deeper, as though if he didn't declare his undying love for her, and soon, the affection fix she so desperately craved simply wouldn't be enough any more.

For the first time in as long as she could remember, she was living in the moment, and loving every second of it.

'Cait.' Dax breathed against her hair.

She lifted her heavy head and looked up into his dark hazel eyes. Her chest rose and fell. Hard.

'Have I told you how sensational you look tonight?' he asked. 'How I've had a hard time keeping from doing something that might get us both arrested for public indecency?'

His words sent a frisson of sexual heat rushing through her veins. It landed with a pulsing thud in the backs of her knees. Oh, yeah. Loving. Every. Second.

'No,' she purred, 'you have not.'

'No? Really?'

Dax looked away. And said nothing more. She slapped him on the chest, her hand bouncing off his hardness before curling into the soft top.

'What?' he asked, his beautiful face a picture of innocence.

'I think you may find you were halfway through a conversation before zoning out there, buddy. Something about my general sensationalness…'

'Fishing for compliments now, are we?'

She laughed so loud she felt several heads turn her way. Including Franny's, which was grinning mushily at her. She lowered her voice as she said, 'You're a bad man.'

'You're dating me, so what's that say about you?'

Her heart did a few extra bumps against her ribs. They were *dating*? That was new. Was it a step up from casual, or simply another word for the same thing? It didn't imply anything exclusive, but *did* leave room for future dates. Okay, she was comfortable with that.

Or as comfortable as she could be while the hand at her hip began to stroke possessively, tugging the hem of her dress up her thigh and down again, his little fingers sliding seductively across the top of her buttocks.

His thumb somehow hooked into the minuscule ribbon of satin that held her underwear on and he stopped dancing. The music throbbed, the dance floor pulsed, and the two of them stood in the middle, staring into one another's eyes, bodies so tight not a slip of light had a hope of blinking between them.

'What *are* you wearing under this thing?' His voice was deep and strained, as if it was taking everything in his power not to slide her dress to her waist to find out.

'Not much,' was all she said. All she could say before her throat clogged with desire.

As Dax's grip upon her tightened he looked at her as if he wanted to gobble her up, and Franny was dead right. That look *was* impossible to resist.

'Let's go,' he said.

'But Franny and Jace—?' Caitlyn said, somehow remembering they weren't the only two people on the earth.

'Are happily comparing their favourite musicals, and can look after themselves. While you and I have better things to do.'

His eyes were so dark she could barely make out their

colour. She swallowed. Nodded. Felt her hand become enclosed in his. He led and she followed as they pressed through the crowd to their table where he grabbed his coat, her purse and her fluffy black jacket, and out of the door they went.

The night air was bracing, especially when compared with the scorching heat of her skin, Caitlyn shivered. Dax slid her soft jacket over her shoulders, but didn't pause long enough for her to put it on. She had to jog to keep up with his long strides.

They crossed the street and headed down a narrow lane, then through an alley cutting between two gothic high-rises. Caitlyn was clueless as to where he was taking her, but he seemed too intent on getting there at such a pace her heel caught on a loose stone and her ankle twisted. She let out a soft 'Ouch!' just as his arm caught her around the waist.

With the sudden cessation of motion her senses came into sharp relief. Their breaths were uneven and strong in the quiet night air, the tall buildings muting the sound of city traffic. A lone bass guitar strummed in a bar somewhere close. Slivers of moonlight filtered through the branches of a pair of a row of trees that had lost their leaves, the light slicing across Dax's jacket highlighting the deep rise and fall of his broad shoulders.

A bone-deep ache suddenly filled her, making her feel heavy and full. As if her skin were too tight, her lungs too small, her blood too thick.

Dax gravitated towards her, and her jacket snagged the concrete wall at her back. She arched away, only to press into Dax, and the hardness against his thigh, which stopped her short. Moonlight now slanted across his eyes. The desire within them hit her as if an airbag had just exploded against her chest.

When he kissed her, or maybe it was she who kissed him, it was hard, lush, deep. Her leg was around his hip, his hand sliding up the back of her skirt. Her mind a swirl of red-hot desire so thick she could barely breathe.

His hand slid to the front, his deft fingers finding their way beneath the barely there underwear with such ease. She gasped as he slid inside her. Her hands gripped his shoulders as he breathed deliciously into her neck, his tongue mirroring the pulse of his fingers. She felt scorching hot and divine.

All too soon every sensation contracted to her centre, her eyes snapped open, the moon round and bright and blinding in her vision as she split apart, his mouth on hers, drowning out the cries of release that felt as if they were pouring from her very centre.

As she collapsed against him, spent, their breaths rose and fell in a ragged cacophony. Cool night air prickled at the perspiration glistening on every inch of her exposed skin.

From the corner of her eye an audience of pigeons pecked at something in the gutter and she realised she'd just let a guy have his way with her in an alley in the middle of downtown Melbourne. What was she thinking?

Her eyes slid to the face of the man who still held her in his arms, and she realised quick smart it wasn't *some guy*, it was Dax. Serious, smart, suit and tie, pillar of the community Dax Bainbridge who looked almost as stunned as she felt at what they'd succumbed to.

'Come home with me,' he said, and as if he'd said the words she knew he meant for her to stay. To spend the night with him. To wake up in his arms.

That wasn't part of the plan. No ho. She fully meant to hold fast to her determination to keep the sorbet sex on home soil, or at least the level playing field of the array of gorgeous hotels and dark secret corners of the city they'd frequented. Going home with him surely meant letting go of control, and that meant giving into the pull of attraction like the junkie she was.

Her mind grew frantic as she searched for an excuse. Or just a plain no. Yet the longer she looked into his eyes, the more the world slowed around her, quieted, paused.

'Come home with me,' he said again, his voice deep, his tone sure, his touch full of promise that she'd not regret it.

'Yes,' she said, not quite convincing herself that the breathlessness that followed was pure and simple desire, and not a bit like the way an addict must feel the moment their drug of choice entered their veins.

Caitlyn stood alone in the centre of Dax's vast lounge room, leaving him asleep in his big bed. She nursed a big glass of tap water in both hands, and stared out at the twinkling lights of Melbourne as moonlight spilled through the wall of twelve-foot-high windows. The cool air of the climate-controlled apartment swirled about her legs, which were bare bar the inch of Dax's old Melbourne Uni T-shirt, which just covered her bottom.

Dax's living space reflected back at her in the smoky glass. All shining dark wood floors and long, elegant, custom-built leather couches. Remote-controlled blinds and recessed TV that slid out from behind the fireplace. She'd found both of those when she'd accidentally sat on the remotes. It was modern, masculine, and immaculate. Much like the man who lived there.

What she hadn't anticipated—in those moments when she'd let herself imagine, knowing it couldn't hurt as she'd never see the place in person—were the small nuances that made him seem all too real. The mud-caked running shoes dumped unceremoniously under the hall stand. The bowl of apples on the kitchen bench that were a couple of days past being edible. The plethora of family pictures lined up on the slick black bureau.

Her eyes danced over the images in the silver frames. There were several photos of a woman who must have been his sister. Laura? No, Lauren. Same straight back, same intelligent eyes, same hairline. There were several of people Dax's age she'd never met. Mates? Cousins? People she'd probably never even heard of. She felt a sharp little pinch in her belly at the knowledge she likely never would. Though, as far as she could tell, there were no pictures of anyone she would have guessed were his parents.

He'd mentioned his folks a few times over the weeks, and every time she'd gleaned a definite tension there, some underlying injury that weighed on him even now, but one he'd never elaborated on. Each time he'd become particularly distant for a moment or two, then brushed past it as if nothing had ever happened.

But something had happened. Something big. Something that had no doubt shaped him into the man he was today. In the past she would have pushed, pried, and prodded until he'd opened up to her, needing to bleed from him every bit of empathy and compassion she could. It was a testament to how far she'd come that this time she'd left well enough alone.

And would continue to do so, she told herself in no uncertain terms. Deep and meaningfuls were way off limits. Way too risky for her susceptible heart.

A glint of pink light reflecting off a photograph shone into her eyes, and she turned back to the windows. The sky was still navy and dusted with stars but the whispers of cloud were turning a faint pink on the horizon.

Morning was near. That was enough to drag her loose-jointed body kicking and screaming back to its senses.

Coming to his place at all had been totally against the rules of sorbet sex, but still being there in the morning would be a punishable offence.

She told her feet to move, but they refused to budge. If toes could sulk, that was what hers were doing as they curled stubbornly into the hard floor.

Aah! If only Dax weren't so exceedingly irresistible. Those intense eyes, those insistent lips, those unholy hands. When he kissed her, touched her, whispered devilish promises of what was to come against the soft spot below her ear, she turned to marshmallow. And not the spongy, sweet, soft kind. The slowly melting-to-liquid heat-over-an-open-fire kind.

In every other thing she'd had with a guy—relationship, fling, whatever—she'd *always* been in the driver's seat. Even while she'd imagined herself being swept off her feet, in the back of her mind a part of her had known she was skewing the relationship in the direction she wanted it to go. *Needed* it to go.

But this time… It felt different. They weren't going down any road she'd been on before.

That's a good thing! she reminded herself. Living in the moment. Having no expectations. It was thrilling not knowing what was awaiting her around the next corner. And, okay, it was kind of scary too.

She glanced over her shoulder towards the bedroom where Dax lay warm and naked and exquisite. All she'd have to do was go to him, to kiss him at the edge of his beautiful lips, or run a hand over his gorgeous backside, and the tumble of thoughts compounding in her head would be lost to her in minutes.

Maybe that was the key to the real success of sorbet sex: to stop overthinking things. To enjoy the freedom of not having to direct every move. To forget the rules and give herself over to their explosive heat. What if it could cleanse her of, not only her grand accumulation of romantic mistakes, but of the insecurities that had sent her hurtling down the wrong path again and again?

Her toes uncurled and walked her towards the open door, towards Dax. Her heart rate quickened, her skin grew tight, and her fingers felt bloodless as her imagination took flight.

And the last thought that slipped into her mind before it was lost to the debilitating blaze of being in Dax's arms was that, even while she wasn't sure what was around the corner any more, she had no doubt that the road she was on with Dax was one she'd never find on any map again.

Dax stirred, the sound of water splashing against a ceramic basin drawing him slowly into the land of the living. He rubbed his eyes and stretched, half expecting to have his heels slipping off the end of a bed that wasn't his.

When they failed to find fresh air, he opened his eyes to find he was in his bed. His room. Yet Caitlyn's sweet scent was everywhere. That was what came of having had her there half the nights that week.

The door to his en suite opened and Caitlyn rocked into the room wearing the kind of extremely high heels that pretended to be business attire while they were really built to turn a man's head. Her fitted grey skirt would also have been perfectly work-appropriate if it hadn't flared into a saucy little frill at her knees. Add to that the fact that she'd yet to dress herself above the waist, and her lacy white bra only just covered that which it was intended to cover, and desire slid hot and fast through his veins 'til it amassed as a beating pulse between his legs.

He willed her to look at him, to smile that saucy little half-smile that told him she was drugged with desire, to crawl down his bed and wish him good morning the best way he knew how.

Instead she sat on the end of his bed, shook her hair over one shoulder and set to attaching an earring to her other ear.

Dax stilled and breathed deep and slow through his nose, suddenly feeling as if he should look away. It had nothing to do with her state of undress; he'd seen her in far less. It was her fingers tugging gently at her ear, and the dainty earring that refused to do as it was told, that had him in their thrall. It felt like a private thing, something purely feminine he'd never been witness to before.

No, it wasn't private. It was *intimate*. Yet while the recognition of such a foreign sensation burned deep in his belly, like the first signs of a stomach ulcer, he found he couldn't look away.

Finally recovering some inner fortitude, he snapped his eyes to his bedside clock, then the book face down on his bedside table, and ultimately the odd dusty handprint on his ceiling.

Intimacy was not on the agenda. Not for him. Not ever. What was the point in letting anyone get that close? Even blood couldn't be trusted not to screw you over if it was in their best interests to do so. If he hadn't learned that lesson hard enough, then he wasn't the man he thought he was.

Duty. Obligation. Accountability. These were concepts he could rationalise. Concepts he correlated with positive results. Living up to and beyond his responsibilities equalled Lauren being happy, the foundation flourishing and the Bainbridge name once more being treated with respect. Outcomes that had led to him finally finding a kind of balance in his life he was happy with.

No. *Content* would be a truer word.

Okay, so he could *live with it*, which was no small thing considering the years he'd spent being furious with himself for not noticing the path of destruction his parents had left in their wake. That he, a man of sense and education, had been so easily duped.

Putting Caitlyn, or any woman for that matter, on some kind of romantic pedestal would be akin to sticking a target on his back, with the word 'SUCKER' written in bold type.

So, if it wasn't intimacy, what was it?

Caitlyn had nothing to do with the other parts of his life, which meant, when he was with her, he rarely thought about anything else. Add the rare lightness she wore like a second skin and he'd never known that kind of effortlessness before. It was bedazzling, and made it easy to forget things. Like work and family. Like real life. That relief from the everyday was a luxury he'd never known before.

It wasn't intimacy. Quite the contrary. It was the beauty of the casual affair. Yes. No question. Much better.

Caitlyn shuffled on the end of his bed. His eyes went to her, the creamy skin of her back, the curve of her waist, the swell of her hips. His body responded as if the beauty of the casual affair had just met a raw and pounding sexual chemistry. The kind that made mere contentment feel like a dirty word.

He pushed back the covers and went to her.

Her profile showed surprise as she was buoyed by his weight dipping the mattress at her back. Surprise and delight.

He wrapped an arm around her waist, nestled his nose into her soft neck and breathed, finding power in the feeling of her skin contracting at his touch.

She hooked a knee onto the bed, and a hand around his neck, pulling him closer even as she said, 'I have to go into work ridiculously early. Right now, in fact. Apparently the delivery of balloons for the launch that turned up last night is the wrong colour and I have to fix it asap. You're coming, right?'

Her hand left him as she set to working at her earring again, a small frown creasing her face.

'Coming?' *Soon,* he hoped, pressing a string of slow kisses across her collar bone. She breathed deep, her skin tightening deliciously with each touch.

'To the Z9 launch. It's on the fifteenth of next month. We've hired the Melbourne Cricket Ground for the evening. It's going to be fabulous.'

The fifteenth was a few weeks away. She clearly imagined they'd still be this into one another by then and the thought of the many luscious nights those few weeks could guarantee slid hot and hard through him.

But the finely honed tug of self-protection that never fully turned off, even with her, stopped him short of making any promises.

Instead he made a move for her still naked ear lobe.

'I have to go to work!' She groaned, pushing him away.

'I'm not stopping you.'

Her brow furrowed as her eyes wandered over him; over his bare chest, over the white sheet barely draping over his lap. When her eyes found his again he could see how torn she was—needing to go, wanting to stay.

It connected with something inside him. An appreciation of those same feelings. Any last lingering doubts curling about his stomach settled. It meant they were both being sensible. Neither of them wanting this to be anything other than what it was.

Then finally her earring clicked into place, and a sigh of relief washed over her, pressing her breasts forward, her head back, and every sensible damn thought fled his head before they were destroyed by a tidal wave of desire.

He took her by the shoulder and tipped her back into

the bed, then leant over her to lay an upside-down kiss on her lips.

What could have been a 'have a good day at work and I'll see you whenever' kiss quickly morphed into something deeper. She reached up to slide her hand into his hair, then used it to pull him closer.

Superhuman strength roared to life within him and he dragged her up and into his arms. There she clung tight, moaning into his mouth as he slid his hands over every inch of bare skin he could find.

When she pulled away, she was breathing so hard. So, he realised, was he.

Neither of them said a word. They didn't need to.

Raging attraction thundered within the amber depths of her eyes and he knew it would be mirrored exactly in his.

She pressed her hands hard against his chest, forcing him down onto the bed. He landed with a thud, the soft feather pillow sinking under his weight.

Her mouth curved into a smile, a knowing smile, a smile full of promise. The groan of desire rumbling through him was so intense it literally lifted his torso from the bed.

She pushed him back down, not once taking her eyes from his as she sourced a condom, fitted him, and strad-dled him. Found him. Taking him deep inside her 'til her breath escaped in a small gasp.

He shuddered, his body thanking her for giving it what it craved so badly it ached.

As she began to rock her dark eyes connected com-pletely with his. Her desire mirrored his. Heightened it. Wrested away his control until he felt as if he had none at all.

Her skirt rode up her thighs. His hands followed its path. All that soft skin beneath his hands and the tightness of her clenched around him was almost too much for him.

Thank God she was as far gone as he, as it was mere seconds before she gripped his shoulders, her head rocking back, her beautiful throat clenching as her body undulated in waves of ecstasy.

He followed, right on cue. Colour and light and awe exploding behind his eyes.

She lowered herself to him, leaning her head on his chest, her light body sinking softly, wholly against him. Her small hand lying gently on his stomach.

He wrapped his arms around her, his head still spinning, his entire body thrumming, sensations too intense to specify bouncing haphazardly about inside the cavern of his chest.

And then something other—something concrete and a million miles away from the sweetness pressing against his life-hardened corners—occurred to him.

'You weren't wearing any underwear.'

'No,' she said, her breath tickling painfully, pleasurably, across his chest, 'I wasn't.'

'Had you intended to seduce me from the outset, or do you often go commando?'

'Now what's wrong with having a little mystery between us?'

Mystery meant secrets. Deception. Yet in that one tiny moment, looking into those melting brown eyes, he wondered if being so unconditionally implacable all the time was excessive. If a little innocent covertness meant more of the kind of action he was still recovering from, maybe he'd been unfair in giving *all* secrets and lies a bad rap.

Maybe the balance he'd found in his life meant he finally had a chance to bend his hard lines a very little.

Maybe this was the girl to teach him how.

CHAPTER SIX

DAX whistled and bounced on his toes as the lift ascended towards Caitlyn's apartment. It was the kind of day that called for whistling, and who was he to deny it?

The Pies had beaten the Blues by a hundred points. The forensic accountants had given the foundation the all-clear. And Franny was…elsewhere. He didn't know where, exactly, and didn't much care. When he'd called Caitlyn's apartment earlier and Franny had answered he'd just made sure she would be somewhere other than there.

Bouncing on his toes, he knocked a tune on Caitlyn's apartment door, imagining her opening it up to him wearing something frilly and sheer. Or a trench coat and high heels. Or nothing at all.

The key turned in the lock and his blood felt as if it were rushing through his system too fast. It needed an outlet. An outlet that was only seconds away.

The door ripped open with such force he braced himself for a soft warm body flinging itself into his arms. But all he got was a whoosh of empty air.

After a moment, he stepped inside and closed the door. Caitlyn was still in her work clothes—wide-legged grey trousers, a fitted pink sweater, and high heels. The thin silver scarf she was unwinding from around her neck made him think she'd just beaten him home. All in all it was no trench coat but she still looked sexy as all get out.

If only she hadn't been frowning up a storm and swearing like a sailor, he'd have been on her in a heartbeat. But she was like a mini-storm, waves of antagonism pouring from her. He planted his feet and forced the adrenalin pumping through his system back under control.

The swearing finally stopped, but the frowning amplified. She sniffed the air and her whole body clenched like it was about to implode.

'Franny!' she cried out loudly enough for the whole block to have heard her. 'If you've made a mess of my kitchen and not tidied up after yourself, there will be consequences!'

And then she stormed into the kitchen, leaving Dax standing, bemused and alone, in the sudden quiet of her wake.

'Right,' he said, to nobody in particular.

Brow tight, he glanced at the front door, chagrined at how recently it had held such promise. And now? Now he had no idea what the hell was wrong. They'd yet to even say hello.

He didn't need this. Not from her. She was meant to be his relief from the pressures in his life, not one more cause of it.

He seriously considered leaving, but the suspicion that she might not even notice tweaked his pride. Besides, his body was a mile behind his head. It was still humming, still neck deep in plans for the evening. Parts of him were still straining towards the vibrating kitchen saloon doors.

Jaw tight, he made a beeline for the kitchen to find Caitlyn pouring a generous glass of red wine. Just one.

'Did we have plans?' she asked, not even looking at him.

A muscle throbbed in his temple. Only pure and utter

stubbornness kept him from spinning on his heel and walking out of her door. He hadn't backed down from bringing up a sixteen-year-old wild child. He hadn't backed down from taking a nearly bankrupt foundation into the black. He wasn't about to back down from Caitlyn's foul mood.

'I had plans,' he said, his tone pointed. 'Specific ones involving you, me, and the contents of your fridge.'

She curled her shimmery scarf around her hands 'til the tips of her fingers turned white. 'I'm not hungry. Where's Franny?'

Not about to give her any satisfaction in knowing he hadn't been looking forward to eating her food, not off the table anyway, Dax breathed deep through his nose, keeping his patience only just in check. 'She made other plans for the evening. Now what's up with you?'

Finally, she looked him in the eye. He braced himself for sass. Or heat. Or some form of the spirit that had kept him there in the first place.

What he got was a shrug. What he got was indifference.

Dax's indulgence gave way with a mighty snap. He'd never needed to push himself on a woman who didn't want him and he wasn't going to start now. The fact that he was so hugely thrown by her reaction only motivated him more to get the hell out of Dodge.

'Fine. Whatever.'

He turned to go, when out of the corner of his eye he saw her flinch. Her face crumbling as if she'd been slapped. This from a woman who always seemed as though she were sailing through life on roller skates.

His back foot anchored itself to her kitchen floor.

Damn it. Damn her!

He slid his hands into the pockets of his suit trousers, and did his best to unclench his jaw. 'What's the problem?'

'Nothing,' she said, shaking her head as if she was trying to shake bad thoughts from it.

'So there's no particular reason why you appear to be on the verge of a temper tantrum.'

She glared at him then, her cheeks blotchy and pink. He tried to console himself with the fact that at least she'd moved on from indifference. But the heat in her eyes was so uncontrolled, so wild, he felt as if someone had jabbed a hot chopstick through his gut.

He didn't like the feeling one bit. Didn't much want to think about what it meant. But he did know the only way to make it go away was to draw out the Caitlyn he'd come to see.

He reached over and grabbed her hand, uncurling the scarf from her cool fingers before she'd wrapped the damn thing tight enough to cut off a fingertip. He shoved it into the pocket of his jacket and dragged her hand to eye level so she had no choice but to look at him.

God, her hand was so cold. And trembling. The chill that had cloaked him from the moment she'd opened her door did a rapid thaw. This wasn't some random tantrum sent to ruin his day. Something was very wrong.

'Tell me,' he insisted. 'Now.'

She shook off his touch and for the first time he felt a frisson of alarm. Was it him? Was this it? *Not yet,* his body urged. *Not until he knew why,* his mind moderated.

'Caitlyn.'

'I'm tired. I'm grumpy. I'd be crap company tonight. You should go home.'

'I'm not going anywhere.'

'Dax!' she said, her voice now rising, panicked even. 'Please. I beg you. I don't know how to put this any more clearly. I want you to leave me alone.'

That could have been it. The end. Perhaps with any other

woman it would have been. But with Caitlyn, this time her very candour worked against her. While her words said one thing, her body told him another. Her eyes were wide with uncertainty, and her small cool hand gripped him so tight her pulse throbbed through his palm.

He slid a finger beneath her stubborn little chin as once more he said, 'I'm not going anywhere.'

She held on for a moment more, her whole body stiff and unyielding, and then, as if a dam broke inside her, her stern stubborn little face just crumpled. And then she started to cry. Not just cry. Great racking sobs that left her gulping for breath.

Dax froze. Stunned into complete stillness before his mind whirred back to life as if it had been spun into the wall of a hurricane from the eye of the storm. Surely this wasn't about him. Then what? Her job? Franny? Her mother? He realised he didn't know enough about Caitlyn's life to know what else it even could be.

Caitlyn's sobs grew so intense she was gulping in breaths, while Dax did a grand impression of an oak tree.

It wasn't as though he'd never seen a woman cry before. Lauren was all emotion and heart and such an adept crier she could have gone professional.

But watching Caitlyn sob her heart out had disarmed him. He felt helpless. Useless. Devoid of whatever sympathy or soul she clearly needed. He didn't do compassion, just as he didn't do intimacy. It was too messy. Too primed for disappointment. Which was why he'd spent years paying others to do it for him.

But he couldn't just stand there, a rampart buffeting all that pain. He might be implacable but he was still human. He yielded just enough to wrap his arms around her, while she resisted and trembled and cried.

After what felt like hours had passed, Caitlyn stopped

fighting and slumped against him, spent, as if the tears had been the only things that had been keeping her upright.

Dax curled his arm behind her knees and carried her into the lounge, depositing her on the couch. He sat beside her, away a tad, but when her soft warm body curled flush and trusting against his, he didn't resist.

They sat that way for some time. Her body curled into his, his eyes focused on some point in the near distance while he tried to think about anything other than how her warmth and gentleness and smallness made him feel so big and strong and good.

'Today's his anniversary,' Caitlyn said, her voice barely above a whisper.

Dax breathed deep, years of living as an island unto himself fighting against the all-too-human need to know. But with the warmth of her soft breath trickling through his shirt, he heard himself say, 'Whose?'

'My dad's. He died seventeen years ago today.'

Dax breathed out long and deep through his nose, disproportionately intense relief that her mood had nothing to with him warring with the kind of tension that gripped him when families were added to the mix.

She didn't appear to have felt his strain either way. 'It was during a rally race overseas,' she said. 'His car flipped a dozen times but that didn't kill him. He got an infection in hospital while in Africa. We didn't even know he'd even been in an accident in the first place…and then it was too late.'

While she melted deeper and deeper against him as the words flowed from her, Dax held tight. He knew all too well the guilt of not being there. The helplessness. The anger. The way it hardened a person. He'd relied on that hardness to cement his success. Though no matter how hard he thought about it, he saw no hardness in Caitlyn. Even in the grip of sadness she was soft, sweet, and strong.

'I *always* do something on his anniversary,' she went on. 'I'll listen to his favourite Springsteen album. Or head up to the roof at work and chat to the clouds. But today—'

He felt the shudder of her next breath vibrate through him, and he clenched so tight he was sure he would pull a muscle within minutes. 'Today?' he repeated, his voice like stone.

'I plum forgot. I went the whole stupid day without thinking of him once. What's worse it took for *Mum* to call to remind me. And I heard it in her voice. She knew. I could feel her condemnation. Caitlyn the great disappointment of a daughter does it again.'

'I can't imagine that's what she was thinking.'

At that Caitlyn perked up, a flicker of her spirit returning. And like fire to a man who'd been encased in ice that flash in her eyes sliced through him, sending waves of heat rocketing through his body.

'Oh ho,' she said, shaking a finger at him, 'you don't know my mother. If they had a rewards card that gave points for disappointing her, I'd be able to fly to the moon and back by now. She was practically *giddy* that I didn't call her first as it's the final proof that even while I'm so *like* him, she clearly misses him more.'

The fire in her eyes raged now, bringing light and life into her red-rimmed eyes. And Dax could maintain his cool no more.

His eyes connected with hers. Desire and heat and something else arced instantly between them. It was recognition. Recognition of past experiences. And recognition of how that could change things.

When the tension became too much, he said, 'Clearly your mother is a heinous cow.'

She coughed, hiccuped, and ended with a bark of laughter before slapping a hand over her mouth.

'What?' he said.

'Don't you dare try to make me feel better. I deserve to feel bad. I forgot about Dad, I'm whinging about Mum. I'm clearly the heinous cow in this scenario.'

'Okay, you've convinced me.'

She laughed again, this time slapping her hand on his arm before it dropped to settle against his chest, a hot little palm print leaving an indelible mark on his skin. On him.

He shifted restlessly on the over-soft chair, until Caitlyn boosted herself upright, giving him some much-needed space. But when his eyes next found hers, eyelashes clumped together by tears, the sweet honey colour so open, so clear, so absorbed by him, he had had the distinct feeling he never ought to have moved. Or stayed.

'I simply wanted to make sure you were okay,' he said, his voice gruff. 'But I understand if you need to be alone tonight.'

The fingers at his chest curled into his shirt, gripping ever so lightly. She didn't need to ask him to stay. And he knew he wouldn't suggest leaving again.

'Do you miss your parents?' she asked.

Dax blinked hard. Apart from the usual platitudes through gritted teeth at Bainbridge Foundation events, he never talked about them to anyone but Lauren, and even then with careful reserve so as not to colour her memories of them. But he was in for a penny now, so what could he say but, 'I have my moments.'

'They died together, right?'

'Light plane. At night. Snowstorm in the wilds of Colorado. Franny,' he said, realising late how she knew.

'Her relationship with Google is not to be denied,'

Caitlyn said with a now familiar self-deprecating shrug. 'What were they like, your folks?'

'Gregarious. Impulsive.' And after a pause, 'Absent. I'd long since moved out of home by the time they died. Saw them rarely as they were always jetting off to some glamorous destination or other. Then that winter they'd dumped Lauren in some random boarding school in middle America so they could head to Aspen for a ski trip. It took me a week to track her down when they died as it hadn't occurred to them to let anyone know where she was. Not surprisingly Lauren did her best to screw up her life after that, as if that's all she thought she was worth.'

And that wasn't even the half of it, he thought, running his thumb hard over a crease in the couch, over and over again, trying to wipe it away. But it was there for good. Indelible.

'It was never part of my grand plan to one day run the foundation,' he found himself saying, as if now he'd started he couldn't stop. 'Or my father's before me, I'm quite sure. I'd put it to him once that he should have the fund run in perpetuity by a wholly unrelated board, but it was too late by then. It had been left to rot. Then he died, and the market stammered, and the only way to keep the foundation from folding was to take it over.'

'So why not now?' she said. 'Why not put in place the unrelated board thing? You're young enough and smart enough to walk away and do something new?'

He looked down at her hair, softly falling from a jagged side part. She clearly had no idea that what he had going on with her was the most 'new' as he'd done in a long time.

'Well,' she said, 'what I will say is that I might have a heinous cow for a mum, but it sounds like your parents were total crap.'

Unbelievably, he laughed. Loud. It echoed off the close

walls of the small room. Usually even thinking about that time made him feel as dense and impenetrable as the centre of the earth. As if he needed to be that tough to carry the weight of responsibility. But now? He felt parts of himself shifting like tectonic plates.

'You're a funny woman, you know that?' he said, slanting a glance her way.

Blushing through a grin, Caitlyn nibbled at the nail of her little finger. Dax found her other hand, turned her palm over and slid his fingers across the soft webbing. Her fingers curled into his touch.

And then she placed a neat leg over his and whatever else he'd been thinking was swept away by a blast of desire.

'Something you want?' he asked.

'I thought now was as good a time as any to apologise.'

'For?'

'Tears, tantrums, family dramas. I know you didn't sign up for that. So, sorry. And thanks. For staying. Though in my own defence I did warn you to go.' At the last she smiled and shuffled closer, her softness gliding against him.

'So you did.' His hands went to her ankle, slipping beneath the wide-cut fabric, kneading their way up the smooth muscle of her calf. She curled and uncurled, like a cat waking from a long hot sleep.

'Anyway, it's all your fault,' she said, her voice growing breathy as her eyes turned dark.

'That I stayed?' he asked, only half paying attention to her words. His fingers had found the soft spot behind her knee, which was going a good ways to putting the past hour behind him.

'That I forgot Dad's anniversary.'

His hands stilled. For only a moment. 'How do you figure that?'

'I was…distracted. I'm distracted a lot lately.'

'It's a busy time, what with the launch coming up.'

She closed her eyes, her hand now playing with the hair at the back of his neck. 'Dax, I was in the middle of an interview with a motoring magazine last week when I had to ask the reporter to repeat her question. I was meant to be thinking about the Z9's chassis specs and instead I was caught thinking about your hands.'

Her words hung between them, thick and seductive. 'My hands are right here,' he said, inching them up her leg until her head dropped back and her breath escaped in a heady sigh. This was what he'd gone there for. This all-consuming heat. 'And if you just stop talking for one damn minute,' he growled, 'you might actually get the chance to live the daydream.'

Laughing, blushing, she lifted her hand to her hair and she stiffened. Her mouth forming a shocked *'O'*. 'No, no, no. I must look a treat. Give me two minutes—'

'Not on your sweet life.'

She made to move.

He stopped her by taking her other leg. He swung it onto his lap and she could no longer be in any doubt as to the heat pumping through his body. 'Didn't I mention my fetish for women with puffy eyes and croaky voices?'

She shook her head.

'Well, then, it seems we both have a lot to learn about one another.'

She coughed out a laugh. 'You have no idea!'

'Really?'

'Oh, no. I think I've put you through quite enough excitement for one night.'

He rubbed the sole of her foot distractedly. She was right. The last hour they'd gone off track, off planet even, but now they needed to move on. And he knew just how.

He asked, 'Free this weekend?'

She tapped her lip, pretending to think. 'Well, I had planned to alphabetise my DVDs...'

He slowly slid his hand up her trouser leg 'til it found thigh. Hip. The edge of a ridiculously diaphanous pair of underpants. His pulse was now bucking like an unbroken horse in a corral.

'Unless I had a better offer,' she said, her voice breathless.

'How does a dirty weekend sound?'

He hadn't realised how dark the room had become until he wanted to see into her eyes. To see what she was thinking. Instead pools of dark honey reflected his own stern face back at him.

'How dirty?' she asked, the timbre of her voice telling him all he needed to know.

Through a smile, he said, 'The family has a place in the Yarra Valley. It's empty, though I can't promise we won't run into a gardener or two.'

'Well, now,' she said, her voice as dark and warm as her eyes. 'If I have the chance at running into a shirt-free, hunky, sweaty gardener—or two—it seems my DVDs will have to wait.'

He nodded. Good. Done. Back on track. The past hour a blip. Forgotten.

'Then as I see it we only have one problem,' he said. 'The weekend is a long long way away.'

His eyes now used to the dark, he caught her smile, and it might as well have been the middle of a sultry summer day for the heat that arced between them. The urge to get her naked found him momentarily stuck deciding which piece of clothing to rid her of first.

And in that pause, a shaft of moonlight found a way between her curtains and landed on her face, and he saw, behind the seductive smile, the merest trace of sadness lingering in her eyes.

Then, abandoning his search for a zip, he gently wiped the smudge of tears from beneath her eyes.

She cupped his cheek, tugged him down and pressed her lips to his. She tasted of warm salty tears, and something unmistakeably her.

Dax closed his eyes, unfit to keep up with the bombardment of sensation that longed-for kiss brought on. All he could do was go with it.

It took for ever until he felt her skin beneath his. The last possible moment before he slid inside her. They made love achingly slowly. Eyes open. Drinking one another in.

There was no denying the new layers of history and understanding and trust brought a whole other level of intensity to their connection. No regretting it either. It was done. It was astounding.

Her hands clutched his back, her gaze boring into his, her need and desire so vivid in her eyes it took his breath away. Then he felt her clench and shudder and he was gripped with a rush of heat and pleasure and release the likes of which he'd never felt. It rocked him deep, ravaging his self-control until he knew if he fought it, he'd be pummelled by it.

As they lay tangled on the couch, limbs entwined, breaths puffing deep, sweat prickling their skin, Dax thought, *Last blip. Last aberration. Now everything would be back on track.*

CHAPTER SEVEN

A DOZEN outfits lay strewn on Caitlyn's bed; sweet summery dresses, sexy skirts and tops, tracksuits with risqué suggestions embroidered across the backside. She stared at them as though she couldn't remember what each one was for. Because suddenly she wasn't sure how she'd got there.

She'd been so angry the day of her dad's anniversary. With herself. With her mum. With her own fixation on Dax. And then he'd turned up, all gorgeous and imposing and overwhelming, and she'd realised that in letting go of control, in living in the moment, she'd undoubtedly allowed herself to become swept up in him in such a way that had made a deeper impact on her life than she'd ever intended.

In the face of all that mixed emotion, she'd felt so distressed, so confused, so trapped, she'd pushed him away. Or at least she'd tried. And when he'd refused to budge...

She groaned in mortification as she put cold hands to her hot cheeks.

But that was then. And now they were heading off for a dirty weekend. And as weekends went a dirty one was surely the best way to negate the other evening—and the tears, and confessions, and unanticipated tenderness that had come with it. *Such* tenderness—

Franny bumped the door open with her backside, both hands filled with steaming mugs of coffee. She came to a screeching halt when she got a load of what Caitlyn was wearing.

'Ah, Cait?'

Caitlyn nodded absent-mindedly, trying desperately to hold onto the image of the skinny jeans and frill-necked top combo she'd just spied in amongst the mess.

Franny's eyes boggled as she stared at Caitlyn and said, said, 'Now *that's* what I call a wardrobe malfunction.'

Caitlyn looked down at the Daisy Duke cut-offs she'd tried on after finding them on the floor in the back of her cupboard. At some point she'd added fringed cowboy boots and a now skin-tight Little Mermaid T-shirt she'd owned in middle school.

'Don't panic,' Caitlyn said. 'I'm not wearing this today. I don't think.'

Franny glanced at Caitlyn's bedside clock and winced. 'Twenty minutes from now Dax will be here to pick you up for a weekend of hot sex and goodness knows what else, so why are you tripping down nostalgia lane *now*?'

Caitlyn slumped backwards onto the only spare corner of her bed and flopped her arms over her eyes. 'I panicked.'

'Why? You've dressed yourself ably for a number of years now.'

'Not for a weekend at Dax Bainbridge's hundred-year-old winery-enveloped, triple-winged, heritage-listed family retreat, I haven't.'

'You've been Googling, haven't you?'

'Like a maniac.'

'Will his family be there?'

'God, no! Are you crazy? This is a dirty weekend, remember. Sorbet sex squared.'

'Pity. That's like your thing. Mums love you. I'm certain it's one of the reasons why guys find it so easy to propose to you.'

'Not all mums,' Caitlyn muttered, shaking her head to clear away that ominous little thought. 'And besides, Dax doesn't have a mum.'

'Poor Dax. Well, I'm sure whatever family he has will love you instead.'

'They well might, in the alternate universe in which I ever got to meet them!'

'Right. Right. Forgot. No family at the family estate. A saucy, sexy, dirty weekend where the two of you can sorbet one another's brains out.'

Caitlyn gave a deep breath and, with renewed vigour, her eyes zeroed in on the pile, cataloguing in an instant what she saw before her, like the Terminator of fashion. She picked out a handful of options, all house-in-the-country sexy as opposed to nightclub sexy, all easily removed.

For the trip down she went with a casually crumpled semi-sheer blue button-down shirt over a beautiful emerald-green camisole. Pale, wide-leg designer jeans. Bronze bejewelled slides and delicate hoop earrings trimmed with sporadic brown beads. Comfortable. Casual. Which was how she'd almost convinced herself she felt until Franny had to pipe up and ask, 'So speaking of proposals, does he know about George, and the rest?'

Caitlyn's fingers flinched so hard her suitcase lid popped open and almost clunked her on the chin.

'What's the time?' she asked, hoping Franny would take the hint and change the subject.

'One minute 'til touchdown. Have you told Dax about George?'

Caitlyn closed her suitcase, and dragged it to her bedroom door before admitting, 'No. Not in so many words.'

Not in *any* words, in fact.

'Caitlyn—' Franny's voice was tinged with a kind of

concern that made Caitlyn's belly ache for some strange reason.

She flapped a hand at her friend. 'All that's irrelevant to what we have going on. It is. Truly.'

Franny opened her mouth, clearly about to disagree, but the apartment intercom buzzed alerting them to Dax's arrival, and Caitlyn was saved from having to talk any more about it.

And in the delicious thrill of seeing Dax, who looked as if he'd stepped out of a magazine ad for country living in his duck-egg blue sweater and chinos, Caitlyn was able to put it out of her mind.

Nearly.

As Dax drove them out of Melbourne and into the countryside towards the Yarra Valley, Franny's question played on her mind.

She wondered if maybe she should tell him about George et al. Perhaps she would, if the right moment presented itself that weekend. They'd be lying naked by a roaring fire, or sipping Long Island Iced Teas on the grand back veranda, or he'd be rowing them across the private lake while she lay back under a parasol reading Tolstoy, and she'd laughingly tell him she had yet *another* confession to make.

He'd be surprised, naturally. But then he'd roll his eyes and come up with some gorgeous reason why he didn't blame them all for wanting to marry her, all the while making it perfectly clear that marriage wasn't in their future and their non-relationship would go on as blissfully as it had before.

'A penny for your thoughts.'

Caitlyn came to with a start to find the tightly packed houses of outer suburbia had become rolling hills covered in waves of yellow grape vines.

She looked across to find Dax smiling at her before his eyes returned to the road, his dark hair lifting and falling with the pleasant spring breeze streaming thorough the open window, sunlight dappling across his superbly cut jaw.

She thought about telling him then. Really she did. But then the belly ache she'd felt at home came back stronger, deeper, and she swallowed it down like a lump of unchewed gristle.

Caitlyn leant back on the leather headrest, tilted her head his way and in her best impression of a six-year-old's whine said, 'Are we there yet?'

He surprised her by slowing down and saying, 'That we are.'

Caitlyn had expected something imposing and grand, like out of an eighteen hundreds English miniseries, all ivy covered stone, animal-shaped topiaries, grandiose French windows, and soot-stained chimney spikes.

Instead what she found was a home.

Nestled amongst well-established trees with branches so wide they met over the middle of the paved driveway, the house itself was two storeys of whitewashed brick and pale grey shutters, beneath a darling slate-grey gabled roof.

On the lower level a wraparound porch skirted the entire house boasting a wooden love seat covered in floral scatter cushions, hanging plants luscious with dark pink bougainvillea, and even a couple of pairs of haphazardly discarded gumboots.

It wasn't until they pulled up to the side of the house that Caitlyn noticed the other dozen cars already lined up in a neat row. European family sedans, luxury four-wheel drives, a couple of imported sports cars, nothing worth under a hundred grand.

Any other time she'd be salivating for the chance to have a closer look. But that day she felt her cheeks burning in panic even as she said, 'Your gardeners sure drive nice cars.'

'Lauren,' Dax said through gritted teeth. Dax's sister's name snapped Caitlyn from her fuzzy panic and fully into the real world.

'She's *here*?'

'They all are.'

'All *who*?'

'Cousins. An aunt or two. The whole extended Bainbridge clan by the looks of it. I'm going to kill her.'

Caitlyn swallowed hard.

Dax shot her a flat smile. 'I told Lauren I wanted the house for the weekend with the express request that she and Rob wouldn't be here. Instead she's ambushed me.'

You? she thought. *Oh ho, no. I'm the one in the net here, buddy!*

'Can we turn around?' she asked, glancing back as if she might be able to turn the car around by her very will. 'Go somewhere else? There was that little motel next to the abandoned petrol station a half an hour back. It looked… like it had vacancies.'

It wasn't until Dax cut the engine that she realised that wasn't going to happen. The head of the Bainbridge family was not the kind of man to cut and run. He took his responsibilities seriously.

'I'm truly sorry,' he said, sliding a hand over her knee, which only added to the scrambling of her brain. 'And I will make sure Lauren is as well, even if I have to hang her out her old bedroom window by the ankles to make sure of it. We'll make an appearance, and then make other plans. Okay?'

The dark gleam in his eyes, the tightness of his jaw, told her how acutely disappointed he was. She could practically see the plans he'd mapped out disappearing before his eyes. Naked, sexy plans.

As if he could read her thoughts, with a groan he leaned in, sliding a hand behind her neck, her hair slipping through his fingers as he pressed his lips to hers. The kiss was firm. If the windows didn't fog it was only due to supreme Swedish engineering of his hulking four-wheel drive.

When he pulled away he shook his head and muttered something about wishing himself an only child. The intensity of his frustration was all that saved her from jumping from the car and making a dash for the road.

'Okay,' she said breathlessly. 'Let's get this over with.'

Dax stood in the shade of a weeping willow, watching Caitlyn let his cousin's kids teach her how to perform the latest dance craze.

Her pale jeans had grass stains from an earlier game of touch footy. Her hair was cascading out of the makeshift knot she'd tucked it into an hour earlier. Her cheeks were flushed. Her forehead creased into a serious frown while she wiggled and twisted and flapped her arms about.

Damn woman, he thought. *Didn't she realise what that kind of wriggling did to his self-control?* His pulse leapt so hard in his left wrist he had to rub at it with his thumb so that it wouldn't spread. All fine and dandy if it was just the two of them, then she could wriggle to her heart's content. But with his family all lurking about, looking as if they had no plan on leaving any time soon, it was just plain cruel.

He felt someone slink up behind him. The only person who had reason to slink was his sister. 'Lauren,' he said.

She planted herself next to him and followed his line of sight. 'So that's what's been keeping you so busy of late. You've been so quiet about this one I was beginning to think she had two heads. Or an IQ so small I'd have enough jokes to keep you on your toes 'til Christmas. Or was a man.'

'It has nothing to do with her. I'm a busy man.'

'Never this busy.'

He refused to look at her. 'You know you didn't need to throw this ridiculous shindig in order to get a look at her. You could have gone through my phone and found her name and number and secretly stalked her.'

'Meow. I didn't realise she was such a big secret.'

Through gritted teeth, he said, 'She's not. It's just…not what you think it is. It's a casual thing.'

Then turned to glare at his sister only to find her smiling beatifically back.

She said, 'Right. So if it's so casual you didn't think it necessary for us to meet her, why didn't you just turn around and go home when you realised I'd pulled a swifty. Off the top of my head I can name a half-dozen inns nearby.'

He opened his mouth to explain that wasn't how he rolled. That he believed keeping things hidden only led to more trouble when they eventually revealed themselves. And today was proof again that secrets always came out.

In the end he thought it best to ignore his sister completely. Unfortunately that wasn't possible.

Lauren tapped a finger on her lip. 'Were you keeping her under wraps because she's not your usual type? Not a cool sophisticate with reptile blood running through her veins. Were you afraid that puppy-dog enthusiasm would cramp your style?'

Dax turned to his sister. 'That's catty, Lauren. Even for you.'

The thunder in his tone didn't make an impact. Not the kind he'd imagined it would. She reared back slightly, but only so that she could get a better look at his face. And then she smiled. Grinned, in fact.

'I stand corrected. Don't get me wrong. I dig that she's everything you're not. Rob's the same for me. He keeps me grounded. While you could do with some lightening up. I like to think of Rob as my counter balance. I wonder if Caitlyn could be yours.'

Dax turned away from Lauren and her searching, smiling eyes. A muscle clenched in his jaw as in silence he watched Caitlyn feign an injury and point to a lounge chair beneath an umbrella. The kids grabbed her by the arm and dragged her back to their game, and with an exaggerated sigh she gave up and gave in.

There was no denying she was different. She was light, bright, and breezy, which was part of what had so attracted him to her in the first place. Though now he also knew that beneath it all she cradled a bruised heart and hid a core of steel. That their similarities ran deeper than their differences.

There was no denying being near all that vitality the past several weeks, work issues hadn't weighed on him nearly as heavily as usual. His constant concern for Lauren had faded to background hum. In fact his life had been looser, simpler, shinier than it had been in years.

He leant against the trunk of the tree, feigning nonchalance while his whole body felt as if it were suffering from the after effects of a Taser attack. It was the strangest sensation. Unnerving. He didn't want to talk about it. He really didn't. But if there was one person in the world who had a chance of understanding...

His voice was low as he said, 'She is different.'

Lauren blinked.

'When people I meet realise who I am I see the moment

their brains begin to tick over as they think, *What can he do for me?'*

Lauren leant her head on his shoulder. 'Been there, brother.'

Dax gave in and wrapped an arm around hers. 'I never had that moment with her. Not once. To Caitlyn I'm not a Bainbridge. Not a walking trust fund or a marriageable name. Not a means to an end. I'm just Dax.'

After a few moments of thick silence, Lauren leant away to look at him, and said, 'Wow. I never thought I'd see the day.'

'For what exactly?' Dax asked, knowing he wasn't going to like the answer, but unable to stop from asking anyway.

'The day the great and mighty Dax Bainbridge, the human oak, would be brought tumbling down to his knees like the rest of us.'

He levelled her with his stare.

Lauren bit her lip to keep from laughing. 'Oh, Dax. If only you could see yourself when you look at her. All mush and goo. It's disgusting actually. But I'm thinking I'm going to enjoy getting used to it.'

He made to tell her there was nothing to get used to, but she gave him a kiss on the cheek and sauntered away, glancing back over her shoulder just in time for him to re-alise where she was heading. Directly for Caitlyn.

He took a step to stop her, and then realised there was no way without making a big scene. He had no choice but to console himself with the knowledge that whatever happened Caitlyn was a smart woman with a clear impression about what they were.

Not able to watch, he ducked around the tree and took off towards the house. On the way Lauren's words echoed inside his head.

He could have turned back. Caitlyn had practically

begged. But he'd found a ready excuse to stay. Because he'd *wanted* Lauren to meet her? Wanted to show her off? Wanted everyone to get a glimpse of what he'd found? How he'd changed? Who'd given him reason to?

He was ripped from his reverie by the sound of Caitlyn's laughter ringing across the lawn as she took off at a sprint, her eyes bright, her mouth wide with delight, her auburn hair flying behind her as she belted over the grass, a handful of mini Bainbridges in hot pursuit, Lauren on the sidelines egging them on.

His feet felt as if they'd been anchored in concrete atop the soft grass. He'd never imagined a future for their relationship. But he was kidding himself if he thought things hadn't long since gone way past even the loosest meaning of casual. Kidding himself further if he didn't admit he was glad.

So what now?

The car ride home the next morning was quiet. Caitlyn figured she had every right to be restrained. She was the one who'd been ambushed, after all.

But while Dax leant his elbow on the open window, his face smooth, calm, as if the weekend away from the city had softened his intense edges, she knew better.

She knew him well enough to know something was wrong. But the real kicker was she didn't know him well enough to feel as if she had the right to ask what that something was.

The weekend had been like a roller coaster from the moment they'd walked through the massive French doors at the rear of the mansion. From the marble-tiled patio a perfectly manicured lawn stretched away into the distance, broken up by tennis courts, stables, an indoor pool house, even a dinky little gazebo.

The patio itself boasted a huge oak table, long enough to seat twenty without a squeeze. With its gleaming white and silver dinner plates, pale green linen napkins, squat vases spilling over with heavenly pink peonies, it had been breathtaking. The kind of beautiful that made your eyes burn from trying to take in every detail so that you'd never forget it.

Saturday lunch at hers had consisted of plates piled with buttered white bread, and a choice of condiments. They were lucky if each condiment got its own knife. Dax's family lunch looked like something out of *The Great Gatsby*.

Then there was Lauren, who had been kind of intimidating actually. Dark and charismatic, just like Dax, but bold where he was quietly confident. She liked Dax's sister; even despite the moments she'd caught Lauren watching her, looking for what she wasn't sure.

And then, later that night, long after midnight when the clan had finally retired, some home, several to the other wing of the house, Dax and she had gone back to their room. She'd been wired from being 'on' all day. But Dax... he'd been quiet.

They'd slept in the same bed. Snuggled even. But for the first night since they'd been together there had been no sex, sorbet or any other kind. She'd thought it fair enough; the house was full of his family, which wasn't the greatest turn-on. But even when they'd woken up that morning Dax had been...distant.

Now, barely an hour into their long drive home, the silence hung over them like a looming rain cloud, low, dark and ominous.

If only she could read his mind. The rare times she'd seen glimpses of the man beneath the suit—like the night at her place when he'd told her about his family, his regrets, his ambitions—he'd been so deeply engaging. There had been moments of real connection, born of a kind of recognition of experiences the likes of which she'd never felt before.

But now she just couldn't get a read on him at all.

Maybe he was just tired. Yeah, surely that was all. Having to foist some strange woman on his whole family couldn't have been easy for him either. Especially someone he wasn't serious about.

Suddenly cold, Caitlyn wrapped her arms about her waist and looked out of her window, trying her best to ignore Dax's reflection in the glass. The face that had been a kind of gorgeous anaesthetic and at some point had become as familiar to her as her own.

So familiar she suddenly recognised his expression intimately. The detachment. The effort. She'd seen it on her own face in the mirror a dozen times before.

He's not tired, she realised. *He's pulling away.*

Her heart squeezed while her stomach tumbled into nausea.

When he dropped her off in front of her apartment building a couple of hours later her muscles were as tense as if she'd been holding the same twisty yoga posture the entire way. Her knees actually cracked when she struggled out of the car, but it wasn't enough to stop her from making a leap for the kerb before the engine even cut off.

When he opened his door to get her bag she yelled, 'I've got it!' Then she slammed the back door and poked her head in through the passenger window.

'Thanks for coming,' he said, a smile on his face that didn't quite reach his eyes.

'It was unforgettable,' she said, trying to smile back, but the pressure of it only made her lungs burn. Awesome. If any more internal organs got involved she was going to be in big trouble.

Then she backed away, fully aware that it was the first time in an age that they'd made no specific plans, no promises to call.

With a casual wave she ran up the steps to her building, pressed in her code and ran inside without a backward glance, her chest actually heaving with the effort at walking away from him.

Heaven help her.

Once inside her apartment, she threw her bags onto her bed, completely lacking the required energy to unpack, then sat on the corner of her bed and stared at a patch of carpet that boasted a blotch of yellow candle wax she'd never got around to getting out.

No time like the present, she thought, sliding to her knees and having at it with her thumbnail. But no matter how vigorously she scraped, or how gently she picked at the edge, it wouldn't budge. It just stared at her: dense, viscous and unpleasantly translucent.

As she sat back on her haunches, actually sweating from the effort to dislodge the ugly mark, as if a plank of timber smacked her across the head she remembered with a painful flash how it had happened.

She'd been carrying a squat scented candle from the lounge into her tiny en suite bath along with a favourite old horror novel and her iPod set to shuffle through a set of decidedly non-romantic Seattle grunge songs. It had been the night she'd broken it off with George.

Back in the present, something else took her over, pressing her to her feet, tugging her towards her chest of drawers.

She reached for the middle drawer at the top where she kept her passport, old keys, a box of spare buttons, every letter and birthday card her dad had sent her from the road wrapped in a tarnished blue ribbon…

And at the very back, tucked behind the tattered remains of her childhood teddy bear, were a small black suede pouch, a red corrugated cardboard box, and a white ceramic poodle that hinged in two.

She pulled them out and opened them. Inside? Engagement rings.

Three engagement rings.

Some kind of compulsion took her over as one by one—for the first time since she'd hidden each far from view—she tried them on.

One was far too big for her, dangling on her finger like a hula hoop. Another was a yellow diamond, which looked sallow against her pale skin. The third, George's, sparkled prettily at her, but its design had clearly been created with a more conservative woman in mind.

As her finger began to overheat, as if it were reacting physically to the very idea of a for-ever-type commitment, she slid them off and dropped them, clattering, onto the chest of drawers. Seeing them together, three in a row, she felt her hands begin to shake. Her cheeks grew pink and hot. Her breaths were suddenly hard to come by.

She slid down to the floor, the handles of her drawers digging into her back, her toes nudging hard against the edge of the sheepskin rug beside her bed.

She'd tried to give them back. She really had. But all three had flat out refused. It seemed she had the knack for finding genuinely great guys. They'd not hated her for how badly she'd let them down. Or maybe they'd hated her so much they hadn't wanted to see the rings ever again.

Her face fell into her hands.

She was a nice person. A good friend. A *great* girlfriend. And a pretty good casual lover, or so she'd thought, until she'd managed to turn even *that* into something else inside her head. Because she clearly had if the thought of never seeing Dax again had her trembling as if she were in shock.

Hadn't she learned a thing? Was she right back there again? The exact same place?

She took a deep breath, several times over, and cleared her mind of the flurry and fear beating against the inside of her skull. Then she let herself own what she felt for real. When she thought of the others, she felt a dull mix of fondness and regret. When she thought of Dax her whole body came to life like a fuse the first time it met fire.

No. It wasn't the same. Though for the first time it didn't feel like a good thing. It felt terrifying.

In the end it was enough to get her off the floor. She tucked the old rings back out of sight and grabbed her sheepskin rug from the side of her bed and threw it over the candle-wax stain.

That night, with some old black and white movie playing unwatched in the background, she painted her toenails inky dark purple.

She could only imagine what Franny might think about that. Probably something along the lines of, 'Caitlyn, my sweet, I think a storm's a coming.'

'I've screwed up,' Caitlyn blurted.

Franny laughed so hard she came to a complete stop on their late afternoon power walk along the banks of the Yarra, pressing her hand into a sudden stitch.

'What did you do this time?' Franny asked after she found her breath.

'It's Dax.'

'Tell me you didn't dump that man!'

'God, no!' Caitlyn's vehemence shocked even her, but then again she had pretty much felt like a walking time bomb since she'd last seen him several days before. There'd

been no saucy little midday texts. No late-night phone conversations that had her drifting into the steamiest dreams of
her life. It had left her shaky and moody and itchy all over.
Her poor body was going through withdrawal.

Power walk clearly not doing a thing to help burn off
surplus energy, Caitlyn flopped onto a sloping patch of
grass by the river and stared up at the sky. Soft puffs of
white cloud meandered slowly across the pale blue sky,
while sunlight flittered softly through patches of new
leaves on the trees overhead.

Usually the path before her had been so clear. Delicious
dating, which led to the exquisite rush of a new relationship, which led to the pure bliss of a proposal, and then…
pure and unadulterated panic. Because she knew better
than to think anything good could last for ever.

With Dax the path was meant to be clearer still. Sorbet
sex then…nothing. But sorbet sex, then dinner, then a double date, then sleeping at his place, then that night at her
place when it had felt more like making love than anything she'd ever known in her life, then meeting his sister…then nothing?

She wondered if even her dad would have relished that
much excitement and adventure. Lying there on the grass
all she felt was a need to lay a hand on her tummy to quell
the nausea.

When Franny flopped beside her with a grunt, Caitlyn
said, 'I thought he liked me,' the words feeling as if they'd
been pulled from her by industrial-strength pliers.

'Duh,' Franny said succinctly. 'And you like him right
on back. Yeah, I see the problem.'

Caitlyn threw a hand over her eyes. 'We weren't meant
to *like* each other. He was meant to be sex without strings.
A way to wipe the slate clean.'

'Cait, you do know that sex might make you forget about

the world for a few blissful minutes, but it won't make it go away. When you come to you're still you, and he's still him.'

'Yeah,' Caitlyn said, scrunching up her face. 'Yeah, I know.' The cool river breeze slid through her light clothing, turning her beads of sweat cold. She shivered.

The whir of bicycles whizzed by on the path behind them, the sporadic call of *Stroke! Stroke! Stroke!* from the teams of rowers sculling their way towards the city echoed in her head.

'So where has all this angst come from? Has he professed his undying "like" of you?'

Caitlyn shook her head.

'Has he written you odes? Sky-written limericks?'

'No. Thank God.' But then neither had he bought her flowers, or chocolates, or jewellery. He'd never romanced her the way the others had, full-out as if they'd sensed she craved mega-wooing. He'd just been, well, him, which to that point had turned out to be more than enough.

'Has he introduced you as the love of his life, the woman of his dreams, his girlfriend even?'

Caitlyn thought back to the weekend at Bainbridge Manor, trying to remember how Dax had introduced her to Lauren and the rest, only to remember that he hadn't. She'd lumbered on in as she always did, introducing herself, not giving him a chance.

'Then relax!' Franny said, slapping her on the arm. 'Maybe he doesn't like you at all.'

Caitlyn shot Franny a glare, which was more than she deserved. Until she realised that Franny had stumbled upon a possibility she hadn't even considered.

What if Dax really was that ambivalent? What if, seeing her with his family, he'd realised it was time to end things before they got messy? What if it was already over and she was just waiting for the fax on Bainbridge Foundation stationery telling her 'It was fun while it lasted'?

All sorts of feelings swirled unimpeded to the surface, so fast she couldn't hope to shut them down. Feelings of loss and sadness and loneliness she'd done her all to block from her life. It was ridiculous! She shouldn't be feeling so blue, so hollow, as if she'd lost something important, because she'd never actually had it at all.

'Franny,' she said, her voice hoarse. 'This is serious. I'm… I think I might…'

Then her phone rang, vibrating against her hip. She lifted her butt off the grass and snuck her phone out of her bum-bag.

It was *him*.

Dax's devastatingly handsome face smiled back at her from the picture she'd taken of him when he'd first given her his private number all those weeks before—face softened with sleep, eyes dark with desire—and just like that the tension building within her for the past three days disappeared. Or more truthfully it didn't disappear. It liquefied, heat flowing through her as if her blood had turned to melted chocolate.

She answered, and pressed the phone—and his picture—hard against her ear.

'Dax,' she said on a sigh. 'Hi.'

Franny pinched her side. Caitlyn looked across at her friend to find her holding her hand to her heart and batting her lashes ferociously.

She swatted Franny's hand away and hugged her knees to her chest. But even she'd heard the longing in her voice.

'My place,' he said, his voice hoarse, as though he too had felt every minute they'd been apart. 'Tonight. Nine o'clock.'

Her skin warmed as if the sun had shone through a cloud

for her benefit alone. She nodded. Then realised he couldn't see her. 'I'll be there.'

'With bells on?'

A smile crept onto her face. 'Kinky.'

She heard his soft rumbling laughter before he rang off.

She lowered the phone and stared at the blank screen. The urgency in his tone had been unmistakeable. His voice had vibrated with it. He wanted her still. As much as she wanted him. Which was a truckload and then some.

The knowledge was empowering. Whatever had sent him into his cave, Dax couldn't keep away from her even if he tried.

Then the obnoxious clearing of Franny's throat reminded her she wasn't alone with her rampaging thoughts.

Franny raised an eyebrow comically high. 'Plans? Kinky plans?'

Caitlyn gave Franny a shove before leaping up and taking off back down the path, a second wind putting wings beneath her feet.

CHAPTER EIGHT

FINALLY, it was the night of the big Z9 launch and Caitlyn had done it! She'd managed to pull off the logistical nightmare of having a circus set up in the middle of the iconic Melbourne Cricket Ground.

Massive red and gold sails flapped above her, while trapeze artists, magicians and fortune tellers roamed amidst the hundreds of gorgeously groomed guests. Laughter echoed through the lofty space alongside the happy sound of tinkling champagne glasses and noisy chatter.

Caitlyn stood in the middle of the floating polished-wood floor with the star of the show, a sleek, shimmering ocean-blue Pegasus Z9. The sports car reposed gracefully on her slowly turning base, all restrained energy, like a jungle cat preparing to pounce. At the right angle it actually looked as if it were on the move.

She imagined herself behind the wheel with the top down, the sun on her skin, the wind in her hair, Springsteen blaring as the supreme machine ground its way around blind corners of a country road.

Her dad would have *loved* it.

She felt a familiar tingle of sadness burn down her spine at the fact that he wasn't there to see it. To see her. To wrap his arm about her shoulder as he always had and say, 'Kiddo, you done so-o-o good.' She crossed her arms across her chest and held the thought in tight; taking every lick of confidence she could from the whisper of a shadow of a ghost of steadfast devotion.

'Do you come with the car?' a deep voice rumbled against her hair.

Her sadness faded like mist in sunshine and with a sigh she leant back into the wall of solid male. 'Depends who's asking.'

Dax's low rumble of laughter created waves of heat like a firestorm rocketing right through her.

She'd hoped he would come, but apart from that first time she'd not mentioned an invite again. It had felt like pushing her luck. Things had been good since they'd reconnected. Better than good. They couldn't get enough of one another, barely using one another's beds for sleep any more. It was hot, heavy, and after dark only. Just how a fling should be.

It was only mildly disquieting that they'd not actually talked about the time apart once.

There had been quiet moments, gentle lulls in between the bursts of heat, when she'd caught Dax looking at her as if he had something to say. But she'd always been the one to drown it out with a touch, a kiss, more. That, added to the long hours she'd worked up to the launch, she'd been left with no time, or emotional energy, to overthink it. To assume anything. Much easier.

But the fact that he was there, supporting her on her big night, was more of a relief than Caitlyn would have dared believe.

She turned into him slightly, enough to enjoy the feel of his hard body brushing against hers, but not enough to let any of the guests think they were in for a whole other kind of show.

'Want one?' she asked, her voice husky.

She glanced up at him, finding herself entangled in the hot hazel intensity of his gaze. Her body reacted as if it had been weeks since she'd seen him, not hours.

'Does it come in red?' he asked, his dark eyes sliding to her hair before moving back to possess her eyes. 'I like 'em red.'

'Because they're faster?'

'Of course.'

'Then this is your lucky night.'

'Promises promises.' Dax's arm slid possessively around her front, tucking across her ultra-sensitive belly, and heat rolled through her until it scorched away any semblance of breath.

She kept turning until they were front to front, his arm now sliding around her back. 'So you'll take one?'

'Of what you're selling? What the heck, I'll take two.'

'My boss is going to love me,' she said, her voice low, her skin a hundred degrees and rising. 'And he's going to want to have your children.'

'Really? Then I'd best get a look at him.'

Biting back laughter, she turned away from him once more, bodies touching, then not, then settling back into the most inoffensive version of a clinch they could manage while still remaining G-rated, and nodded towards the bumptious man with the ruddy cheeks and exploding belt-line chatting loudly bellow the trapeze trampoline.

Dax said, 'He looks like he's on the verge of a heart attack.'

'Not your type?'

He gathered her closer and into her ear said, 'Not even close.'

As if he knew he was being talked about, Caitlyn's boss frowned deeply, creating new chins beneath the old ones. He turned, sharp eyes seeking out the perpetrator, when

he spotted Caitlyn. It was only in that moment that she realised that Dax was wrapped about her as if he were her
own personal man-shaped coat.

She felt a blush rising, and slapped at Dax's arms.

But it was too late. Her boss shook the floor as he made
a beeline their way. Then his face broke into the first real
smile she'd ever seen him make.

She swayed back as she said, 'Mr Crispin, this is my…
that's to say this is—'

'Bainbridge, right?' her boss said, practically drooling.
'Eli Crispin. Great pleasure to meet you.'

'Likewise,' Dax said, not letting her go while he reached
around her to shake her boss's hand. 'You've got yourself
a winner here.'

Eli's eyes went straight for the Z9 and he nodded profusely. 'Isn't she a beauty?'

'I was talking about the party planner, actually.'

He glanced at the top of Caitlyn's head. 'Yes, yes. Fine
job. Exciting night. Now tell me what you think of the
fender. I wanted it to be reminiscent of the Bespoke Racer
yet with a contemporary edge.'

Crispin flapped a substantial arm at a wandering drinks
waiter who all but lost his tray as he did a fast one-eighty
turn in order to serve the boss.

Caitlyn quickly disentangled herself, only to have Dax
glare silently and wrap a hand about her wrist. The most
innocuous of touches yet it burned through with the fe-
rocity of a reckless kiss. And even that had nothing on the
intensity in Dax's eyes.

Her heart beat hard enough it took her breath right along
with it. Then with a quick spin she managed to loosen his
grip and step back. Away. Space the only way to defuse
the obscuring sparks zapping between them.

She mouthed, 'You'll be fine,' then spun away and walked off as fast as her heels could carry her.

Whether it was the heat of his touch or the intensity in his eyes that had her feeling unsteady, all she knew was she needed to cool down. She had a job to do tonight. She'd deal with the rest later.

After what felt like hours later Caitlyn found a spot behind the fortune teller's caravan to rub the balls of her feet.

'Cait, this is amazing!' Franny, late as to be expected, said as she tracked Caitlyn down, drink already in hand. She gave her friend a hard one-armed hug. 'I reckon if you asked for a freebie right now, they'd give you the Z9 of your choice.'

Caitlyn laughed. 'Yeah, right. Have you met my boss?'

Franny scrunched up her face. 'Good point. You might be in for a free ham at Christmas if you're really lucky. And in the spirit of getting lucky, how's Dax? Is he the life of the party, or what?'

Caitlyn glanced across the marquee. As if he had a homing beacon secreted under his skin, she'd known exactly where he was all night. Some of her best clients—superegos all and frustratingly impossible to charm—were crowded around him, listening intently as if he were some kind of rock star.

For a guy who didn't do the party scene he looked as if he'd been born to woo a crowd. Tie-free in a white shirt and grey linen jacket, he oozed effortless sophistication like nobody she'd ever known. It came down to confidence. And if there was anything sexier than a man being comfortable in his own skin she hadn't found it yet.

As if he'd felt her eyes on him, Dax's eyes found hers. He stopped talking mid-sentence, oblivious to the chatter that broke out around him. In that moment she doubted there was anything sexier than Dax Bainbridge, full stop.

She had been looking forward to this night for months. It was the most important night of her career. It was an absolute triumph. And suddenly she couldn't wait for it to be over.

'Honestly, no man should be allowed to be that beautiful. It's unfair to the rest of them.'

Caitlyn blinked and glanced sideways. She'd forgotten Franny was even there. 'Sorry. What?'

'Your guy. He's lovely, Cait.'

He is, she thought. *Beautiful. Brilliant. Built to last.*

A waiter slid discreetly by. Franny grabbed him by the cuff of his sleeve and piled her napkin with assorted hors d'oeuvres. Caitlyn shook her head. Apart from not wanting to end up with parsley in her teeth, or onion breath, she had so much adrenalin rushing through her fuelling a toxic mix of desire and dread, doubts and dreams, she couldn't stomach a thing.

'Hey, I keep forgetting to ask,' Franny said, 'what happened when you guys *finally* had the "previous relationship talk"?'

'We've as yet to traverse that minefield,' came a deep voice from behind them.

Caitlyn blanched, spinning so fast her heel caught in a tuft of grass and she had to grab a caravan tail-light to stop from landing on her backside, while Franny almost choked on a crab puff.

'Why do I get the feeling if I'd waited another minute I'd have walked in on something really juicy?' Dax asked, his dark eyes filled with assurance, not suspicion. Not even a little.

'You have no idea,' Franny muttered.

Caitlyn shot Franny a quick glare, but Franny was steadfastly ignoring her.

'I see. So what are we talking about here?' Dax asked, now glancing from one to the other. 'A string of broken hearts leading all the way from the Central Coast to Melbourne?'

'Well—' Franny began, until Caitlyn kicked her in the shin.

As Franny bounded on the spot, grabbing her leg, Caitlyn said, 'Sorry. Thought there was a bee on my foot.'

Franny raised her eyebrows manically at Caitlyn, encouraging her like mad to get it over with.

But when she told him, *if* she told him, about George and the others, it would be when the time felt right. Not here. In public. At the most important work function of her career.

Frowning madly back, Caitlyn said, 'Unfortunately I signed non-disclosure agreements with every single ex. Reasons of national security.'

Dax's dark eyes collided with hers, questioning but still not wary. 'That juicy? Now you have me intrigued.'

'And for tonight you'll just have to stay that way. Remember how much we decided we like a little mystery?'

'Did we now?'

Franny had stopped choking, only now her eyes were all but bugging out of her head. Caitlyn ignored her as best she could. Hoping her friend would get the point and move on.

She did. Franny spun on her heel and took off, leaving them alone. Just Dax, Caitlyn, and her past, which suddenly felt like an anvil around her neck.

And she knew the fact that she was working, or in public, or wearing green for that matter, had nothing to do with her decision to hold off telling him.

It had far more to do with the look in his eyes as he'd watched her all night. The same look she'd first seen the last time they'd been together. She'd woken during the night to find Dax watching her, his dark eyes roving over her face. It had made her feel special. It was a feeling of such intimacy, and connection, and trust, like nothing else she'd ever known.

But if he knew about George, and the rest, she felt certain he'd never look at her as if she was such a prize again.

She swallowed. Hard. Feeling as if she were all at sea without a lifeboat and the sharks were circling.

'Mingle with me?' she said, grabbing Dax by the hand and yanking him out into the safety of the crowd.

He curled her back to the caravan's shadow. 'There are other things I'd rather be doing with you, which don't include hordes of strangers.'

She avoided his eyes. Tried a joke. 'You are so-o-o straight.'

'Immovably so.'

As his breath warmed her skin, she so wanted to lean into him, to soak up all that gorgeous male warmth. But all the thoughts of boyfriends past had created a barrier around her, as if she were wrapped in cellophane.

'Caitlyn! Miss March!'

Her boss's voice split the heavy silence and she was so relieved she could have wept.

'Duty calls!' she sing-songed, avoiding Dax's astute eyes as she ducked under his arm and walked away. Fast.

After she'd given her boss the directions to the men's room that he'd been after, Caitlyn tracked Franny down, grabbing her by the elbow and physically walking her away from the Pegasus interior fabric designer she was flirting with.

'No!' Franny said, looking longingly over her shoulder. 'He was the one. I just know it.'

'He's married.'

'Damn it!'

Caitlyn manoeuvred them to a secluded spot behind a massive potted palm tree, her eyes scanning the room to make sure no one was within hearing distance. 'Franny, I beg you to be more circumspect.'

'About what?'

'Talking about me, private things about me, while I'm working. In front of Dax.'

Franny was so shocked she looked as if she'd been kicked in the shin and for no good reason this time. Then her face cleared of all expression until it was eerily blank. She wiped a smudge of sauce from the corner of her mouth and said, 'You mean how you've been engaged three times.'

Caitlyn nodded shortly, not looking at her friend.

'Jeez, Cait, I can't believe you haven't told him yet!'

'I— It's no big deal. I haven't told him I kissed Kyle Manning behind the science lab in grade five either. Or that I got to second base on school camp in grade twelve with a boy whose name I haven't been able to remember in years. Or that I, a grown woman, had a little crush on Zac Efron during the whole *High School Musical* phenomenon.'

'We're not talking about a crush or two. I'm talking about George. And Alex. And…Whathisface with the dimples and the chocolate Lab.'

Marty, Caitlyn thought, *I was engaged to him for two days after dating for a month. No wonder my best friend can't remember the poor guy's name.* She pushed the memory away. 'It's complicated.'

'No,' Franny said sharply, shaking her head in Caitlyn's peripheral vision. 'It's really not.'

A shiver of something familiar, and awful, scooted down Caitlyn's back. She and Franny *never* fought. In fact Caitlyn never fought with anyone. Probably because of the tangled push and pull of her relationship with her mum, she was a cheerleader. A peacemaker. The idea of disappointing someone who loved her brought her out in hives. So much so she'd never once said no when someone perfectly nice and completely wrong for her had asked her to marry them. While Franny was just impossible to offend.

'Can we just drop it?' Caitlyn asked as her neck grew hot and patches of skin started to itch.

'No. I don't think we should. The way I see it, if you and Dax are exclusive then he deserves to know.'

Caitlyn felt an urge to put her fingers in her ears and shout 'lalalalala'.

'So you're not exclusive,' Franny said.

'Not…expressly.'

Not that she'd seen anyone since she'd started dating him. Or wanted to for that matter. The very idea seemed unnervingly ludicrous. And the idea that he might be out there dating other people made her feel physically ill.

'So what is he? How have you described him here to-night to anyone who's asked? What if old Crispin wanted to know? Is he your boyfriend? Your friend? Your booty call?

'Franny—'

'Because the thing is, Cait, if he is just a casual screw, as you're still trying so desperately to convince yourself he is, then how can it possibly hurt for him to know?'

Franny's harsh language shocked Caitlyn from her es-calating catatonia. She spun to face Franny, mouth open wide. Then realised she had nothing to say.

Franny took her by both hands, forcing her to look her in the eye. 'He's not the kind of model you replace once he's exceeded his warranty. Dax Bainbridge is a keeper. On any planet. And as far as anyone with two eyes and a modicum of smarts can see, he adores you to the ends of your oft-coloured toes. If you want him, he's yours.'

Caitlyn wished there were a chair nearby. If she didn't

put her head between her knees, and fast, she was going to faint.

Because Franny was right. So right. Dax was nobody's rebound guy. Nobody's sorbet. He left far too lasting an impression to be considered anything nearly so insubstantial. In fact she felt pretty rotten inside for ever allowing herself to pretend she'd ever believed it of him.

Dax Bainbridge was beautiful, brilliant and built to last.

One problem: *she* wasn't.

She'd tried. She really had. She had the engagement rings to prove it. But when it came to the crunch she crumbled. The thought of committing herself to one person, to promise to love one person for the rest of time while armed with the knowledge that it could all be taken away in the blink of an eye, gave her panic attacks.

'I need…more time.'

'For what? To break up? To ease up? To realise what anyone looking at you can see in an instant—that you're awesome together?'

'I don't know.'

And that was a startling truth. Usually she plundered forward in order to avoid looking back. But now she had no idea which way to turn.

Maybe she'd broken the pattern after all, only the catharsis she'd been searching for didn't come. If anything she felt worse. Franny wrapped an arm around her and gave her a great squeeze. 'Oh, hon. Just know I'm only ever looking out for your best interests. And if I didn't give you a polite slap across the back of the head if I think you need it, I couldn't call myself your best friend. Okay?'

Caitlyn nodded, not trusting her voice.

Then Franny gave her a big kiss on the cheek. 'I'm going to mingle. Find myself a lonely millionaire. Think about what I said, okay?'

When Franny slipped away, Caitlyn's vision cleared and she realised her boss was now waving madly to her, and jabbing his pointer finger at a pair of well-dressed boys who looked as if they were just out of high school and worth a billion dollars already. Tech nerds. Just her crowd.

She took a couple of moments to bring her breathing back under control. To find a way through the emotional vacuum sucking up every feeling in its path.

She rubbed her cheek, knowing Franny's bright red lipstick would have left a mark, and with her head high she plastered a smile on her face and got back to work, knowing the internal marks their conversation had left would take a lot longer to fade.

Dax found himself alone for the first time all evening, conversational muscles aching from the kind of networking a marquee ripe with testosterone brought about. He took the opportunity to discreetly stretch his stiff cheeks.

And to watch Caitlyn. Her strapless green cocktail dress with a shimmer that caught the light. Her smoky eyes. Her silken hair.

Two young men nudged their way into the circle of prospective clients milling around her. One gave her champagne, which she accepted with a friendly smile before launching back to her story.

He felt a proprietary thrill that the cashed up young bucks could use whatever moves they had at their disposal; but she'd still be going home with him.

After the weekend at the manor he'd made the executive decision to cool it with Caitlyn. Things had become rather more...*intense* than he'd ever intended them to be. That was something he'd done a bang up job of ignoring until Lauren had forced him to admit it. In the time apart he'd taken stock, re-evaluated the bounds of their dalliance. Something any businessman worth his salt would do if contract negotiations were on the horizon.

It had been one of the hardest weeks of his life, and that was saying something. He'd been crotchety, hard-assed, quick to temper. Everything had felt off kilter, prickly, and wrong, especially the parts of his life that he'd believed had finally achieved balance.

And that was because the time and space had only given him room to see that it hadn't been balance. It had been resignation. He'd decided his life was what it was and that was that.

Which had been sufficient. Until Caitlyn. He hadn't understood the full extent of the impact she'd made on him until he'd felt the lack of her.

She'd found a way under his skin, deep in his bones. She'd entwined herself inextricably with his deepest desires. But only because he'd let her.

It had been a scary thing, letting her get that close. He'd found it virtually impossible to trust much of anything after his parents had proven to him how well even those closest could hide the darker parts of their nature.

But the more he knew of her, the more he was certain that Caitlyn *was* different. What you saw was what you got. And what he got was an open, honest, fragile, funny, sexy, impertinent woman who made him feel—

He felt so much, far beyond anything he'd ever known, that he breathed in hard and deep through his nose to quell the unfamiliar rise of emotion. But even the cooling night air did nothing to still the warmth that beat through him at the sense that if he played his cards right there were as many nights with her in his future as he wanted.

In the distance Caitlyn laughed; one hand closing around her throat, another slapping riotously against her thigh. She shook her hair from her face and Dax imagined the feel of it slipping through his fingers: soft, silky, and warm.

He imagined the taste of her skin as he scraped his teeth over the ridge of her shoulder.

He imagined the sound of the zip of that saucy little dress grating against his taut nerves before it pooled to the floor, leaving her in nothing bar whatever sliver of underwear she had on and those crazy, sexy high heels.

He imagined that hot, languorous look she got in her eyes in the last moment before he kissed her. Each and every time. As if he were all she'd ever been waiting for and more.

As if she could perceive the power of his feelings, her gaze swept to him, caught, and she didn't look away. Even from that distance he could see the extreme rise and fall of her chest, could feel the restraint it took for her not to brush away her groupies and come to him.

How many more nights did he want with this woman?

He wanted them all.

As Caitlyn kiss-kissed the last of the guests goodnight, she could feel Dax waiting for her. She looked around until she found him leaning on the bar. She caught his eye, and gave him a quick frown of apology.

He nodded.

A nod wasn't usually something she read much into, but that nod was different. It was serious. It was intense. It literally gave her goose bumps.

All she could put it down to was that he must have been mulling over their conversation by the fortune teller's caravan all damn night, wondering about the ghosts of boyfriends past. She sure had. She could all but hear them whispering to her, *Tell him. He's a good man. He deserves to know what kind of woman he's mixed up with.*

Caitlyn looked away to frown at her shoes. She wanted to smack Franny. She really did. If only Franny hadn't already gone home with one of the billionaire tech nerds Caitlyn would have found a way to shake her friend 'til her teeth rattled. Of course Franny might have hooked up with both tech billionaires. The thought of Franny's disappointment when she discovered they only spoke Klingon at home was small consolation.

'Night, Cait.'

She smiled and waved to a bunch from the engineering lab whose night had clearly only just begun.

'Wanna come?' One of them did a horribly intoxicated version of the twist, which she assumed was an invitation to go dancing.

'Thanks but I—' She glanced at Dax again. He was watching her still, his face a study in shadows. The sudden urge to party with the engineers was a strong one. But the magnetism of the tall, dark, gorgeous man waiting for her was stronger still. 'Next time, okay?'

They waved and blundered away.

No, tonight was not a night for dancing. Tonight had brought to a head the knowledge that she'd managed to get this far into her thing with Dax without getting hurt, or hurting anyone else for that matter, by sheer luck alone.

She needed to slow things down. To give herself some real room to think. To decide once and for all what she and Dax were to one another. Because all she was really sure of was what they *weren't*.

He wasn't a booty call. He wasn't a casual acquaintance who shared her bed every now and then. From the moment they'd first touched they'd never been so awfully dry. And he wasn't so wholly unimportant to her that she could tell him the least flattering stories of her past and not care what he thought.

'Everything okay?' Dax's voice echoed in Caitlyn's ear.

She blinked to find all of the guests were gone. The tent was empty bar a cleaning crew who had materialised from nowhere and were busily wiping away any sign that they'd ever been there, so by that weekend the ground would be as ready for a game of Aussie Rules football as it had ever been.

'Yes. No. Fine.' Caitlyn shook her head, not knowing the answer. Just knowing she felt a sudden desperate need for fresh air. Air that didn't smell so deliciously of clean laundry and fresh cotton and pure soap. Of Dax.

'Ready?' Dax put a hand on her waist, but, rather than sinking into it as she usually did, that time she flinched. Her reaction must have been so out of the norm, and so obvious, as Dax's hand was suddenly gone.

A napkin scattered past her feet in the suddenly cold breeze. The beep beep beep of the truck reversing to take the Z9 home to bed split the night. She risked a glance at Dax to find him staring hard at his shoes, a muscle clenching in his jaw. He was a bright guy. He wasn't immune to her mood.

'Not ready quite yet,' she said, her voice strained. 'I ought to do one last sweep to make sure nobody needs anything. But it's late. You go ahead. I'll be fine. I'll call you tomorrow. Or next week at the latest. Because I'll be super swamped. Tonight we wooed. Tomorrow we strike. Okay?'

It was rubbish. A lame excuse to prolong the inevitable conversation she knew she had to have about who she was. And what she'd done. Eventually. Soon. Weeks ago.

Suddenly she felt mentally and physically exhausted, so drowsy she could barely see straight. Her knees buckled under the weight of it and she swayed. Naturally, Dax caught her. He was just that kind of guy.

He swore beneath his breath, his arm wrapping tight around her waist. 'You're shattered. I'm taking you home.'

'Smooth talker,' she mumbled.

He laughed, and shook his head, his eyes finally connecting with hers. 'Whatever did I do in my life to deserve you, Caitlyn March?'

She swallowed, and tried to look away but couldn't.

At the tone of his voice, the glint in his eye, her body found some latent untapped well of energy. The urge to slide her hands beneath his coat and rest her cheek against his hard chest, selfishly absorbing every bit of his latent heat and strength she could, was staggering.

Get some space, she reminded herself, *slow down. Back away from the beautiful man! Whatever you might have done in the past you always had the will power to do the right thing when you truly needed to. That time is now!*

Somehow she gathered every bit of strength she had left in her weary body and eased away. An inch was all it was, but an inch away from Dax might as well have been a mile for the pull he had over her.

'Come on,' he said, his voice deep, rough, gorgeous.

Her eyes caught on his, but all she saw was the reflected gleam of the stadium lights. He jutted out an elbow and she slipped her hand through, the contact at once too much and not nearly enough.

In silence they took the long walk through the MCG grounds and onto the city street in which she'd parked so many hours before. When they reached her latest Pegasus company car, a cruisey little sedan in rocket-ship red, their steps slowed as one.

She turned to Dax, arms crossed to stave off goose bumps pricking up all over her skin even beneath her warm coat. The words 'Goodnight, Dax' danced on the tip of her tongue, but the look in his eyes stopped her short.

Franny had said he was hers for the taking, and, standing there in the muted moonlight with the noise of the Richmond train station clattering in the near distance, Caitlyn wondered if she might be right.

Her eyes flicking from one of his to the other, she felt herself bombarded with emotion. With affection and desire, and something else so big, so powerful, she didn't dare attempt to name it, knowing how wrong about that kind of thing she'd *always* been in the past.

Unfortunately, not naming it didn't stop her feeling it. Feeling as if her skin were being pummelled with a million warm raindrops. As if her bones had turned to milk. As if he were filling every nook and cranny of her being until her entire body pulsed.

Dax reached out, slowly this time, and ran his thumb over her cheekbone, as if he was waiting for her to flinch again. She didn't. The sensation of his skin sliding against hers felt so good. Too right. He gently tucked a strand of hair behind her ear. He rested his big, warm, protective hand on her neck.

Then he leaned in to kiss her.

Time, space, and slowing down entered her mind for a split second before her lips met his with the most gentle of contacts. Then just like that she lost the fight.

She pulled him close, and kissed him hard. As if a dam had broken inside him his kiss became brutal, fuelled by an avalanche of yearning the likes of which Caitlyn had never known.

Fear and confusion and logic were pulverised beneath the combined forces of their desires and in their place was a ferocious rising heat that no one small person could ever hope to contain.

Only when a horn sounded over and over as a car of

laughing drunken louts roared by did they pull apart, breathing heavily.

She rested her forehead on Dax's hard chest, her shaking hands on his waist. He felt so heavy against her, as though he needed her strength to keep himself upright.

After a long, long while, Dax slid a finger beneath her chin and lifted her face so that she looked into his eyes, and, while the moon had gone deeper behind the rows of feathery clouds drifting across the sky, she could still see every nuance in his dark gaze.

And like the addict she clearly was, and would be until the end of her damnable days, she stood there and lapped up every last bit.

'Caitlyn—' he began.

She placed a finger on his lips and said, 'Take me home.'

CHAPTER NINE

CAITLYN stared at her face in Dax's en suite mirror, and barely recognised what she saw.

It had nothing to do with the dark smudges of day-old eyeliner and exhaustion under her eyes, or the tangle of knots making a mockery of what had been sleek and sophisticated hair the night before. Neither was it the red marks peeking out from the neckline of Dax's borrowed T-shirt from where he'd nipped her shoulder, or the swollen appearance of her lips, which felt bruised from the hours upon hours of kissing.

It was something deeper. Uglier. It was the knowledge that while sex the night before had been breathtaking, mind-numbing—it had been sorbet sex.

Caitlyn rolled her shoulders and lowered her gaze, literally not able to look herself in the eye.

There was no kidding herself now that every other time she'd slept with Dax it hadn't been about forgetting what had been before. It had been about being with him. She'd been swept up fully, by the thought of him and the reality of him, from the first moment she'd seen him, touched him, wanted him.

But last night, faced with the probability that her efforts to break the dating habits of a lifetime might mean pushing

Dax away before it was too late, she had used sex to forget. Only, this time, the man she'd wanted to forget was him.

She heard a rustle of sheets and a deep masculine groan from the next room. Her shaken gaze shifted, catching Dax in the edge of the mirror as he stretched his muscled arms over his head, his large feet nearly poking off the end of his huge bed. He ran long fingers over his face, then through his hair, creating a mess of spikes.

The best sex of her life. The only man who'd never let her get away with anything. The only man strong enough to keep her honest. The best man she'd ever known.

She rubbed her knuckles across her chest, about the spot where her pathetic excuse for a heart ached. No wonder. It was a feeble, sorry thing, weakened by too many missteps, too many false starts, too many direct hits.

'Morning, sunshine.' Dax loomed suddenly behind her, sweeping her hair aside to lay a warm kiss on her neck.

'Morning,' she scratched out.

'I have something for you.' His voice was deep and throaty, making her skin tingle and her hands clench on the sink.

Whatever he had she didn't want it. And she wanted it more than life itself. If she had one working nerve left at the end of the day it'd be a miracle.

'So long as it's a long shower and a toothbrush, I'll take it,' she said with false brightness.

'Well, then, lucky for you…' His arm slid around her, and in his hand, tied up in a big black satin bow, was a new red toothbrush. For her. To leave at his place.

Her hand shook as it reached out and curled around the plastic handle.

'Red,' she said, the only word she could manage while her heart coughed and spluttered and tried to spark to life, but the fractures merely widened until it threatened to shatter for good.

'Of course it's red. Red's faster.' Then, 'Coming in?'

She blinked into the mirror to find him standing by the shower naked. A god.

Her mouth went dry at the thought of being hot, wet and slippery with him. But the toothbrush, and what it represented, was burning too significant an impression into her hand.

She backed away slowly. 'Maybe later. I'm ravenous. Going to whip up some breakfast.'

'Make mine a double.' He gave her a kiss on the nose. Then, as his eyes grew dark he pulled her to him and kissed her more thoroughly on the mouth.

She closed her eyes tight as she fell into a well of desire. At the edges of her subconscious something deeper and warmer ebbed gently through her.

She snapped back to reality as Dax spun her around, gave her a pat on the backside, and sent her padding out of the bathroom.

Once in the kitchen, she placed the toothbrush carefully on the bench, not letting it out of her sight for long as if it might rise up and bite her if she didn't watch it closely enough. Clearly she was delirious. No wonder. She hadn't eaten a thing the night before, and had been far too busy doing other things all night to sleep a wink.

She'd be able to think better with a full stomach.

Scrambled eggs, she decided when she realised Dax had little else in his bachelor-friendly fridge. But no matter how many of the trendy deep drawers she went through, or frosted-glass cupboards, or doors that swung open and concertinaed closed, she couldn't find a pan, much less a whisk.

She opened her mouth to call out when she heard the shower turn on.

A thin drawer tucked away in the corner was her last hope. She slid it open. She'd never have noticed a whisk even if it was hot pink and covered in glitter as her eyes had snagged unwaveringly on something else: a small black velvet box. The very same size in which one would usually find a ring.

Her heart jerked so suddenly she could almost feel the fractures splintering into a thousand tiny little pieces, like a crystal orb that had been lobbed from a great height onto a slab of unforgiving concrete.

But even as her body went into a state of shock, she reached for the box, her fingers curling around the soft edges as she pulled it out of its dark hiding place and into the light.

It was meant for her, of that she had no doubt. She'd seen the look in Dax's eyes the night before. She'd known what it meant. Hell, she'd dated the guy for the past few months. She'd been right there as they'd grown closer, become more intrinsic to one another's lives. But no matter how often she'd swapped her metaphorical blinkers for the next size up in an effort to deny it, her chickens had just come home to roost.

Damn it! Damn him! She'd never asked for this. She'd specifically told the guy she only wanted something casual. She'd been so careful to seem cool and uncompromising, even when she hadn't felt it. To make him think she was cruising along, even when she felt her armour slip time and again. To not let him know her inevitable weakness for men who cared, and most specifically her even deeper weakness for him. And now…?

Infuriation—white hot and resentful—propelled her towards Dax's bathroom where the air was now thick with steam, or maybe that was her mood. She slid open the shower door in a rush.

The sight of him all soaped up and tanned, his beautifully sculpted muscles shining and wet, was almost enough to have her turn on her heel, put the ring back and pretend she'd never found it. Pretend everything was peachy.

Dax washed soap from his eyes and saw her standing there. He grinned a wolfish grin. Then his eyes found the ring-box teetering on her shaking upturned palm and the smile slowly faded away.

'I was looking for a whisk,' she said, her voice rich with accusation. She jabbed the velvet box at him as if it were evidence of a war crime and not something she had, on occasion, gone weak at the knees for.

Dax turned off the jets, pulled a large folded chocolate-brown towel from the rack above his head, and wrapped it around himself as he stepped from the shower. He said, 'The whisks are in the canister on the bench.'

'Dax—'

'It's for you by the way,' he said, motioning to the velvet box with a tilt of his chin.

Her mouth snapped shut and she closed her eyes, her whole world turning blood red. She took a deep breath, opened her eyes and tried again. 'Dax—'

'Would you care to open it?' he asked. Watching her carefully.

No, she didn't want to open it! Because this time it didn't feel as if she were on the crest of some fantastical romantic wave. This time she didn't feel that all-consuming rush of adrenalin.

This time she knew it was the beginning of the end.

No more late-night phone calls that sent her wild. No more lunch-hour strawberries and champagne in gorgeous hotel suites. No more Dax.

Suddenly she struggled to breathe. The mist in the bathroom wasn't helping, and neither was the fact that Dax was half naked, his presence and scent and heat filling every inch of the small room.

She turned on her heel and moved to the relative vastness of the bedroom. The bedding was a shambled mess. The imprint of her head was still on his spare feather pillow. Had they really made love for the last time?

She felt Dax follow. His singular scent curling around her, making her body ache for him, for what she'd lost. For what he'd thrown away!

Unless…

This had never been like before. They'd made up the rules as they went along. Maybe they could still.

She spun around, words clogging her throat at the sight of him running a small towel through his dark hair, muscles working in his arms, his stomach. A cruel reminder of all that was fast slipping away.

Realising the ring box was cutting into her tightly clenched palm, she uncurled her clawed fingers and slowly put it on the bed. Dax's eyes followed, narrowed.

'We have a good thing going, don't you think?' she asked, drawing his attention back to her.

'Clearly.' His intelligent eyes swept over her clenching and unclenching fingers, her feet that couldn't keep still.

'Then why change things?'

'Because things change.'

'But we promised we'd be casual. We promised no strings.'

His eyes connected with hers. 'That's what people say in order to protect themselves from the possibility their date is a stalker. Or lives in a house full of teddy bears. Or is bad in bed. I think it's safe to say we both lucked out.'

'Dax—' she began, but he cut her off.

'Caitlyn, I never wanted strings with anyone else.'

And her mouth snapped shut.

Then he walked to her, water sliding down his neck creating shiny rivulets around the muscles of his chest. She felt so faint from the mix of desire and panic she had to breathe through her mouth.

He wrapped his hands around the tops of her arms. His touch calmed her, warmed her, and damped down the worst of the panic. And, like metal to a magnet, her eyes slid back to his.

'Caitlyn, sweetheart,' he said, his voice deep and tempting, 'I've spent my whole life not letting people get close to me, not trusting those who've tried. Until one night a stranger felt me up on a dance floor and everything changed. You, my gorgeous girl, dragged me kicking and screaming out of my cave that night, and every night since, and you brought me into the light. Your light. Your candour, and sweetness, and joy, and strength. Your willingness to give anyone a chance to know the real you despite knowing full well how it feels not to have that warmth returned.'

He swept a hand over her hair, then the other, before cradling her face between his hands until there was nothing between them but breath. 'I'm in love with you, Caitlyn.'

Caitlyn's breath bled from her lungs in an intoxicating rush as her Achilles' heel stretched and preened like an overindulged cat.

Dax. Dax Bainbridge. Big, beautiful, invulnerable Dax Bainbridge was in love with her! She felt as if she were on the brink of everything she'd ever wanted. All she had to do was reach out and grab it.

But her hand wouldn't budge. It simply refused to move

as emotion clogged her throat, and beat achingly against her ribs, and crackled painfully over her skin.

And she knew why.

It didn't matter how he thought he felt because he didn't know what he was asking of her. He didn't know her track record with love. With commitment. And it was all her fault because she'd been remiss in telling him.

Why hadn't she told him? Because she'd thought he *wouldn't* love her if he knew? Or because she knew her experiment was doomed from the start? Because deep down she knew the reason she'd chased love with such fearlessness, such unabashed vigour, was because she'd known she simply didn't have it in her. to catch it.

She felt things, for sure. But love? No. Nope. Couldn't. Wouldn't. She'd built up such a resistance to the real deal she'd finally become immune.

And if the promise of Dax Bainbridge wasn't enough for her to change her ways, no man was. She was destined to be alone, and at twenty-eight, *man*, was that a hard truth to discover.

A sense of cool overcame her, starting in her toes and ending at the points where Dax's warm hands held her. She could see him, feel him, but suddenly it was as though she were looking at him from the wrong side of the looking glass.

Dax had come to love her. She was a lost cause. It was only fair he knew it.

'Dax,' she said, her voice now unwavering. She waited in utter stillness until she had his full attention.

'Yes, Caitlyn.'

She had to swallow, twice, before saying, 'You see, the thing is…' *Here goes*. 'I've been engaged before.'

He became so quiet. So still. All that tightly leashed power that usually simmered just beneath the surface now coiled deep down inside him like, like the energy at the centre of the earth.

'Engaged,' he repeated, the word sounding heavy on his tongue.

'To be married. To another man,' she said, not wanting to leave him in any doubt.

'When?' he asked, his jaw clenched.

Oh, God. This was going to be awful. Far worse than it had been with the others. The pain tying her gut in knots was nearly unbearable. Because he meant more to her? Probably. Not that it mattered a lick.

'Five years ago.'

Dax's nostrils flared and his dark eyes swept from one of hers to the other. She knew he was shocked yet trying to be understanding. And she wasn't even halfway through her confession.

Her heart rate tripled, her skin throbbed, then on a half-choke she said, 'And two years ago.'

'Twice,' he said, his forehead creasing, his breaths coming harder. 'You've been engaged *twice* before?'

She nodded. Then shook her head. Her body came over all numb, as it attempted to protect itself from the horror it knew was coming.

'Caitlyn?' he said, his voice dark.

'Three times,' she croaked, feeling like such a fool as she admitted as much out loud. Then, as if she were about to tear a Band-Aid off as fast as she possibly could, she scrunched her eyes shut and blurted, 'I broke up with my last fiancé George earlier this year.'

When she opened her eyes it was to find all the light gone from his. And whether it was putting a name to one of the men she'd dumped, or the timeline, she'd never know. But Dax's hands finally dropped away, and so suddenly she stumbled, catching a hold of the edge of his bed with the backs of her knees before she fell.

The man who'd as yet never let her fall didn't even notice.

Dax blinked. And again. Yet still he felt as though he wasn't seeing straight.

One moment he'd been staring down the barrel of the kind of future he'd never imagined he'd have for himself. And the next…? Boom!

He breathed deep through his nose as the reverberations shook through him. Everything he was feeling, everything that was happening, was all new territory for him so he had to make sure he was completely apprised of the situation at hand before proceeding.

Caitlyn had been engaged. Three times before. Okay. That was a bombshell, to be sure. The idea of *any* other man coming with five feet of her made every muscle clench 'til it burned. But worthy of the hot sickness currently eating at his insides?

His eyes swung to Caitlyn's, glinting slowly but surely back into focus to find her sitting primly on the edge of his bed, so still, so cool, she appeared practically catatonic. But her eyes… They were wide, panicky, and sorry.

And then he knew. As if a fist had clamped around his heart and squeezed 'til he saw the truth, he knew what his gut was trying to tell him.

It was no accident that this was news to him. She'd kept it from him on purpose.

Caitlyn had lied to him.

And he'd never even seen it coming.

He looked away, the bitterness boiling in his gut hitting his veins, blistering beneath his skin until his whole body felt hot, prickled with sweat.

The shock of his parents' self-serving lies had played havoc with his place in the world, with his family's name. He'd grown from a boy to a man with the hard work he'd put into piecing those things back together until they were stronger than ever before.

But this? This was personal.

That Caitlyn had hidden such a large part of her make-up from him and got away with it struck at the very foundation of the man he'd built himself to be.

That early lesson had taught him never to trust first impressions. To never take people at face value. To believe everyone had an agenda. Yet, for her, he'd softened, swayed, let himself believe maybe, just maybe, she was different. In the end she was no better than any of them, choosing what to reveal about herself, and what to conceal according to how it would best benefit her. And he, a grown man of thirty-six, with an MBA and a multimillion-dollar company under his reins, had just been hauled back to square one.

Just like that the heat sizzling through his veins dissipated, and with it came a hardening cool. This time he'd learned his hardest lesson, not as a boy, but as a man. And this time he'd damn well never forget it.

He glanced up to find her face an illustration in unhappiness as she looked into his eyes. Pain flickered to life deep down inside him but he slapped it down so fast it shrivelled up, whimpering in a dark cold corner.

He didn't care. Not any more. Not ever again. Fortified by *that* truth, he looked her dead in the eye. 'Deep down I think I knew it all along.'

'What?' Caitlyn asked on a sigh, as if she'd been holding her breath the whole time.

'I knew you were too good to be true.'

To her credit she didn't even blink. Didn't look away. It was almost as if she took his words as punishment deserved. 'I'm sorry you think that. But to be fair I never pretended I was good.'

'No. You just pretended to be honest.'

This time she flinched as though he'd slapped her, and he felt it ricochet with an ache as if he'd been kicked in the groin. He gritted his teeth.

'I never pretended to be good,' she said, her chin tilting a fraction, 'and I certainly never pretended to be perfect. I'm a woman with a past who has made mistakes and I'm sure I'll continue to do so. And you're no walk in the park yourself, you know.'

'I never lied.'

Life sparked into her eyes, bright and burning. Her nostrils flared, as though she were ready for a fight, but she swallowed her next breath, then slowly licked her lips before saying, 'Can you honestly say that every second we were together you told the absolute truth?'

'Of course.'

'What a load of rot!' Fidgeting now, she turned so that her knee angled towards his, bare beneath his oversized T-shirt that barely covered her thighs, and shook her head. Her hair fell over her shoulders in great rumpled waves. Dax felt himself getting aroused. He slapped it down.

'Everyone lies,' she insisted, 'either by omission, or timing, or simply not to hurt someone else's feelings.'

'Is that why you held off on telling me about your plethora of failed engagements—so as to not hurt my feelings?' His eyebrow rose slowly as if to say, *Me? Hurt? Ha!* He wondered if she believed it.

It certainly caused a reaction. She bounced off the bed as if the spark in her eyes had swept through her. 'Yes,' she said. 'No. Maybe I didn't want my feelings hurt. I don't know. But now you do know.'

She threw her arms out in surrender, as if that was all she had.

Well, he'd hit the end of his rope too. 'Now I know,' he said. 'I know I never really knew you at all.'

She half laughed, half sobbed. 'Stick you and my mother in a room together and you can surely find a million reasons why I shouldn't win person of the year. But give me a break. I'm just trying to get by in the world using the limited emotional resources I've been dealt. Just like everyone else. Just like you.'

He'd had enough. He didn't want to hear it. Didn't want a discussion. Didn't want a consensus. Fool him once, shame on her. Fool him twice and he'd never be able to look himself in the eye again.

He stood, found a pullover and jeans on top of the leather couch in the corner of his bedroom and pulled them over his still-damp body.

'Dax, wait. Don't do this. Talk to me, please. Ask me anything. I'll tell you the God's honest truth.'

Anything? He knew he should leave but there was one last anvil hanging over his head. He'd been ignoring it until that moment, pressing it to the back of his head since this whole conversation had begun. He'd told her he loved her and she'd never said it back.

He turned to her and, unable to keep the raw edge from his voice, said, 'Tell me how you feel about me.'

Her honey-brown eyes pleaded with him not to go there, to let her off the hook. But he was done prevaricating. 'I want you to say it,' he demanded.

She swallowed, hard. Her eyes blinking fast, her chest rising and falling as she gulped in great difficult breaths. She took a step his way and the familiar scent of her hair slid beneath his defences, the gleam in her beautiful eyes hooked him through the middle.

Tell me!

'I want you, Dax. You know I do,' she said, and for a brief blinding moment he believed her. Until her face slowly lost all colour and she added, 'I just can't promise to want you for ever.'

Caitlyn stared at the ring box in her hand. Somehow she'd ended up with it again when she was sitting on the bed. The damn things gravitated towards her like homing pigeons.

She held it out to him, her hand shaking as if it weighed a tonne. Dax stared at it as if it were a bomb with a lit fuse, before his eyes swept back to hers, dark, cold, empty.

And in that moment she knew there was no fixing things. No going back to the way they were. No more making up the rules as they went along.

She waited for the usual relief to flow through her, but it never came. Perhaps it was all too raw. Too sudden. Too soon. Far too soon...

'Dax—' she choked, tears clogging her eyes, her throat.

But he didn't want to hear it. He stormed from his bedroom, grabbed his keys from where they'd landed when he'd thrown them in haste the night before, then took a dozen long strides to his front door.

Caitlyn followed on numb feet. In fact her whole body felt numb. As if it were made of ice. Dax stopped. His body practically vibrating with the effort. When he turned his hazel eyes were as dark as coal. 'I should thank you.'

'For?'

'Not waiting until further down the track before proving me right.' He dropped his head. Shook it once. Then said, 'We're done, Caitlyn. I'll be back in an hour. When I get back I want you gone.'

And with that he left.

Out of his apartment.

Out of her life.

And while she tried to tell herself that she'd done the right thing, that she'd found the will power to do the right thing at the right moment, she didn't feel changed, or grown-up, or vindicated for having broken the patterns of a lifetime.

She felt empty. Alone. Lost. As if the implosion of the relationship were like a supernova, obliterating her emotions until they were now nothing more than specs of space dust floating in a vacuum.

She wondered if how she was feeling right now was anything near how the others had felt when *she'd* walked away. If so, she deserved it. Every damn bit.

CHAPTER TEN

LAUREN stood in the doorway of Dax's office, arms crossed, not looking happy about something. For once Dax ignored her. He simply didn't have time to care. Feeling a need to be categorically certain, he'd asked to see the latest string of benefaction proposals before allowing them to go through, which had meant working day and night.

She sighed.

'Not now, Lauren,' he growled, frowning at the PDF that was blurring before his exhausted eyes.

'Yes, now,' Lauren said.

Dax lifted his eyes and glared at her.

She glared right on back. 'I was in the IT lab looking for Rob, when I overheard a couple of the accountancy girls outside the door. One of them was near tears because you'd gone rank at her for something she hadn't even done. What the hell's going on with you?'

He set his teeth and stared past his sister to an unframed picture hanging in his assistant's office. It was some rubbish modern art thing that was worth a mint. One of the first investments he'd made while dragging the foundation out of bankruptcy with his bare teeth. As investments went it had been smart. Suddenly he couldn't stand the sight of it.

'Fine. I'll apologise to her. Is that all?'

When Lauren said nothing, Dax glanced up to find her

staring at him hard. Then something she saw made her face soften. She closed the door behind her, ambled inside, then smoothed her skirt beneath her backside as she rested it on his desk. 'So spill. What's wrong? Your favourite suit at the cleaners? Grammatical errors in every proposal? Love life gone awry?'

He felt the muscle beneath his left eye twitch.

Lauren sat bolt upright. 'What happened? You kids have a fight?'

He looked back at his computer where the words had melted into one another. 'Caitlyn and I are no longer seeing one another.'

'No!' Lauren cried. 'What did you do?'

Giving up, he closed his laptop. 'What makes you think it was my fault?'

'You're the man. Of course it's your fault.' Lauren bit her bottom lip and looked honestly upset. 'I know I busted your chops, but I liked her. Best of all I like how much you liked her. I really thought she might be a keeper.'

'As did I,' he admitted, yet the hitch in his voice surprised even him. He frowned even deeper. Emotion had no place in his life. Anger, disappointment, fear, love... Gone. He was a husk, a successful workaholic husk, and it suited him just fine.

Lauren's face fell. 'Oh, Dax. What happened?'

Dax shook his head. 'It doesn't matter.'

'It does to me.'

The need to be Lauren's rock, to be the one stable influence in her life, was a hard habit to break. But as she sat there, so straight-backed, and married, and level-headed, he realised that his little sister was all grown-up.

He picked up a round paperweight filled with bubbles, then leant back in his chair and looked at his sister as an equal. 'She wasn't who I thought she was.'

'Pfft. Who ever is?'

Ignoring Lauren's outburst, he continued. 'It appears that she had been affianced before.'

'Oka-a-ay.'

'Three times.'

Lauren's eyes widened, but she said nothing for a while as she let that gem soak in. 'Married?'

'Not so far as I know.'

'Well, that's something. But come on, Dax, are you really that surprised only three guys have fallen in puddles at her feet?'

'Four,' he said before he'd even felt the word forming. He cricked his neck. *In for a penny...* 'I'd bought a ring.'

He ran his finger and thumb over his tired eyes. He'd been walking down Collins Street when he'd glanced through the window of the antique jeweller and there it had been. The thing had just screamed Caitlyn, glinting so prettily and joyfully from its bed of velvet, as if it had been made for her.

'Show me,' Lauren said, hand outstretched.

'It's not here. In fact I don't know where it is. She might still have it for all I know.' He shrugged. What did he care where it was? He never wanted to see it again, much less think about it, or her for that matter.

He leant forward on his chair, ready to tell Lauren to shove off, when she asked, 'Do you want me to get it back?'

'What back?' Dax asked, rubbing a hand over his tight neck.

'The ring. I'd be happy to go over there and demand she give it over so you can get your hard-earned dosh back. Spend it on a holiday to Ibiza, or another grey suit, or a flash new car. Girls like flashy cars, you know. Especially the kind of girls who make break-ups easier to forget.'

Dax breathed in deep and attempted to picture himself

with such a girl. He really did. Instead his mind drifted to the image of Caitlyn draped over the bonnet of a sleek, curvaceous Z9. A red one. Caitlyn liked flashy cars. No, she liked cars in general. It was one of the cool things about her. And when he was with her she'd made many things easy to forget.

Frustration and regret stabbed him through the gut in ferocious strokes. So much for being a husk. But he'd get there. Another few all-nighters chained to his desk, reading through application after application for money, would be enough to drain any man of all sensation.

'Dax,' Lauren said with an insistence that made him think it wasn't the first time. 'The ring?'

'Leave it be, Lauren. Please. I'm a big boy. If I decide I want it back then I'll get it back.'

The word 'if' hung on the air between them. But only he knew what it really meant. Whatever other unpleasantness had gone down between them, the ring had been meant for Caitlyn. It wasn't his to return.

Finally, Lauren pushed herself off his desk and planted a kiss atop his head before sashaying towards the door. Once there she turned. 'You're so darned decent, and honourable, and you hold yourself and everyone around you to such high standards.'

'Thank you.'

'It wasn't a compliment, Dax.' She gripped the door handle. 'I'm saying it must have taken some guts for her to tell you about the others when she did, knowing it might blow up in her face.'

'Lauren,' he growled.

She held up a hand.

'Just put yourself in Caitlyn's shoes. She's had some pretty spectacular fails when it comes to relationships, and that kind of thing leaves chinks in a girl's confidence. I know. Then she meets this guy. A guy who is sort of funny, and urbane, and okay-looking I guess. A guy who clearly likes her back. That's scary stuff for a girl with chinks. Marry her, don't marry her, but at the very least give her a break. And give yourself one while you're at it.' She nodded towards the pile of papers teetering on his usually impeccably neat desk.

He stared at her then, this smart, sassy, astute woman who had appeared as if out of nowhere.

Then Lauren said, 'I, of course, know the apparent vision of perfection sitting before me is all a ruse. And if she's half the girl you thought she'll have figured that out too.'

With that she knocked twice on the door before disappearing into the foundation's halls.

Dax flipped open his laptop and stared at it blindly for a good several minutes. Then, looking for a distraction, he went through his desk, yanking out drawers, looking for something to do. Anything hard and laborious and boring he'd been putting off for a rainy day. Pens rattled to the front of one drawer before landing softly against a fold of delicate silver silk and satin, and his breath lodged in his throat.

Caitlyn's scarf. His dry cleaners had found it in his suit jacket a couple of weeks back. It was the one he'd shoved into a pocket the night she'd cried in his arms.

The night she'd opened up about how much she missed her father. About her difficult relationship with her disillusioned mother. The night he'd told her about his parents. About professional aspirations he'd barely even shared with himself. The night they'd made love on her couch, tenderly, staring into one another's eyes, both knowing it was against the rules for both of them.

He pulled the scarf from the drawer. The scent of her hair rose up to tempt him. He wrapped it around his fingers, the shift and slide reminding him too vividly of her sighs as she took him inside her.

He wondered if she'd gone looking for the scarf. If she'd remembered he still had it. If thinking about him made her feel as rotten as he felt thinking about her.

Then he remembered as clearly as if she were standing right in front of him the look on her face when he'd told her it was over. Once he saw past the glorious dishevelment and half nakedness that haunted his dreams still, the look on her face was so forsaken it could make a lesser man cry.

Then Franny had called once at the start, trying to plead Caitlyn's case. Telling him she'd always got over past break-ups with panache but this time she was a mess. He'd gritted his teeth and reminded himself that things had never been as they appeared. He'd thought her the one, to her he was one of many.

And maybe that was where the biggest problem had been from the outset. He'd mistakenly thought her different. She'd clearly thought him exactly the same. And for the both of them that had never changed.

'Damn it all to hell,' he said to nobody in particular as he shoved the thing to the back of the drawer.

His assistant poked her head in the door.

With a grimace, he waved her away. She'd been with him long enough to know it was best to shut his office door.

On the outside it was just the same as it had been after George and the others; three in the afternoon on a Saturday, Caitlyn slumped under a blanket on the couch, still in her pyjamas, toenails painted black, Franny supplying her with endless hot chocolates and slasher flicks on DVD.

But on the inside she couldn't have felt more different. Relief hadn't come on the day and it certainly hadn't come in the days since. Loss, anger, and disappointment had overcome her in waves. And yearning. So much yearning. She missed Dax to the point it throbbed within her like an open wound.

God, why couldn't she just get over him already?

It was over. He'd made that perfectly clear. And she knew it could never last. So why was she feeling so uncomfortable, so prickly, as if a colony of ants had taken up residence in her stomach?

She threw the blanket from her legs. When she stood up her feet had pins and needles she'd been sitting on her backside for so long. On wobbly legs she tottered to her bedroom.

'Just so you know I've made my last hot chocolate,' Franny called out after her.

'My waist line thanks you!' Caitlyn called back.

In her bedroom she slumped on the side of her bed. Her eyes slunk to her bedside table. She picked up the small black box that had been living there, unopened, for over a week. She hadn't been able to hide it away in the chest of drawers with the others. The others might have been her dirty little secrets, but this one felt…different.

Before she could stop herself, she slid her thumbnail into the groove and tilted. The soft sound of the hinge working might as well have been fingernails running down a blackboard for the prickles it sent scooting down her spine. A sparkle of reflected light hit her in the eye. She tilted the box to find a bed of creamy beige velvet, tucked into which was a diamond ring. Her hand shook as it fluttered to her throat, as if that could protect her from the emotion that swarmed through her at the sight.

On a band of white gold a modest solitaire sat nestled in a flourish of curling petals encrusted with a trillion sparkling pave set diamonds. It was just lovely. Utterly joyful. This from a man who claimed he never really knew her at all?

A sparkle hit her right eye once more, and for half a second it felt like an extravagant version of a metaphorical lightbulb. As if the universe was trying to tell her something—

Then the feeling came back in her feet and she cried out.

A few moments later her bedroom door creaked open and Franny's head poked through. 'You okay?'

Caitlyn waggled her feet to fend off the sharp pain of blood flooding back into them. 'Actually I think I am.'

Franny's glance dropped to the ring and stayed there while her feet brought her into the room. 'Sweet ring.'

'Isn't it?' Even Caitlyn heard the sigh in her voice.

'Way more you than the others.'

'I was just thinking the same thing.'

Franny's face screwed sideways before she slumped next to Caitlyn on the bed. 'Tell me again why you said no?'

Caitlyn's eyes slid back to the ring, which glinted prettily up at her, as if it were basking in the sunlight. Enchanted. Carefree. Happy. It occurred to her that wasn't the ring she was seeing, but the feelings that lit her up from the inside when she was with Dax.

'I didn't say no. I never gave him the chance to ask.'

'Right,' Franny said. 'Smart move.'

After a long pause in which the birds outside Caitlyn's window were the only noise, the bedspring creaked as Franny shifted. 'But you do love him, don't you?'

Caitlyn's eyes squeezed shut. God, how she loved him! It was like a whirlwind inside her, fast, furious and breathtaking. How could she not? He was handsome, funny, sophisticated, sweet, sexy as hell. Only such a man had a chance in hell of breaking down every barrier she'd put between herself and even the possibility of love.

The kind of guy who was strong enough to tug her back in line. Confident enough to not let her get away with the crap she usually pulled. Who never jumped just because she'd asked him to. A man amongst men, Dax was, and she'd let him get away.

'Yeah,' Caitlyn said, 'I do. I love him. Not that it matters now.'

'Why the heck not?'

'He's my comeuppance.'

'He's not an avenging angel, Cait. He's just a guy.'

'Just a guy? Dax Bainbridge is no more *just a guy* than he is sorbet. He's the best thing I've ever had in my life.'

Not as if she'd told him though. Even when she'd had the chance. Even when he'd outright asked. In that moment she'd turned to stone, riddled with pure fear. Fear of loving and losing and wanting so much and not feeling as if she deserved it.

Franny slid a comforting hand around her elbow. 'He's also just a guy who loves you.'

'Past tense.'

'Do you really think he could switch it off so fast? Could you?'

Caitlyn knew that he could have dumped her in sky writing in front of her friends and everyone and her body still would have burned for him. 'But I'm not him.'

'Thank goodness for that. I mean, imagine the wedding pictures. Odd.'

Caitlyn laughed for the first time in days. It lasted half a second before her heart squeezed so hard she thumped the heel of her hand to her ribs to counteract the pain. The kind of pain she'd spent her adult life trying to avoid. The pain of loving someone with all your heart and losing them anyway. Yet there she was, feeling it to her very bone marrow.

And surviving. Yet again.

She blinked into the afternoon sunlight, searching desperately for the glimmer of…something the ring's sparkle had set alight inside of her. And finding it. Bit by bit, inch by inch, the fog that had descended upon her starting to clear. If she was ever going to move on with her life, for real, not just for fun, she knew what she had to do.

She dragged herself to her feet, her legs wobbly from lack of use.

'Whoa, there, partner.' Franny stood and held her by the elbow.

Caitlyn took a moment to ground herself. She wiped her eyes and rolled her shoulders and headed to her cupboard. *Take no prisoners*, she thought as she zeroed in on a clean pair of jeans, a white T-shirt, a navy blazer, and simple silver flats.

She pulled her hair back into a no-nonsense ponytail before putting on her war make-up. She was going to need all the confidence she could muster to do what she had to do next.

'Where are we going?' Franny asked as Caitlyn brushed her teeth with as much vigour as if she were prepping for a Colgate commercial audition. 'I know! Let's head to Shangri-Lovely and get you perked up. Your toenails have been black for a week. It's unhealthy. They look like they've been trodden on. I'm thinking a hopeful colour. Yellow. Like a bright new day.'

'Sounds like a plan. But first I have something else I have to do.'

Caitlyn stood in front of the charming Fitzroy terrace house, her knees shaking as badly as if she were about to visit the Queen.

The Queen might well have offered tea. If the man behind the door even opened it to her she'd be shocked to the soles of her feet.

She glanced back at the car. Franny sat at the wheel, nibbling at her fingernails. She put on a bright smile and gave Caitlyn a thumbs-up when she realised she was being watched, though she looked exactly how Caitlyn felt. Panic-stricken.

Only, Caitlyn knew something Franny didn't. Feeling things, even the strongest of things, wasn't going to kill her. So long as she was absolutely honest about what she was feeling, then she could get through it. It turned out she was far stronger than she'd ever imagined she was. She wondered briefly if her mum would be proud of that tough streak. She ought to be, it came from her.

Caitlyn's hand still shook as she wrapped her fingers around the brass knocker. She willed him to be home, because she knew she couldn't get on with the rest of her life until she put this chapter behind her for good.

The door swung open.

'Caitlyn!' He was shocked, for sure. But he no longer looked as if she'd torn out his heart.

An honest smile spread across her face as she said, 'Hi, George. I know this is a surprise, and I'd fully understand if you want to shove me down the steps, but I'd really like to come in for a chat.'

Her ex-fiancé breathed deep as he watched her, as a dozen different emotions played across his kind face, but something in her eyes seemed to calm him down. He frowned a bit, smiled a bit, then shook his head as if he'd seen it coming all along.

'What?' she asked.

'It's nice to see you, is all.'

Such a super guy, George. She remembered how much fun they'd had and how she'd liked him a hell of a lot.

But compared with what she felt for Dax? Just thinking his name made her heart crumple and her blood bubble and her skin tingle like the hottest summer sun beating down on the roof of a car. What she felt for Dax was...everything. And more.

'Come in,' George said. 'Coffee? Coke? Beer?'

'All of the above.'

As she crossed the threshold of her old boyfriend's house her hand went to her bag where his engagement ring—and two others—sat neatly tucked, ready to go back to their rightful owners.

The fourth ring, a lovely flower of diamonds that made a person smile just to look upon it, was back at her house, safely hidden under her pillow.

First thing Monday morning Dax stood up in front of the Bainbridge Foundation board while Lauren gleefully handed out the prospectuses he'd spent the weekend perfecting.

'Ladies and gentleman,' he boomed, dragging their attention from the papers and back to him. 'You may have gathered by now that I have before you a proposal to take the Bainbridge Foundation into its next and, I believe, best incarnation.'

Mutters and denials and much kerfuffling erupted, until Dax stilled them with open palms, and a full explanation of why he was stepping down, and how he believed the time had come to let his grandfather's legacy be the only hold the Bainbridge family had over the foundation.

He caught Lauren's eye mid-speech. He expected to see her grinning, like the co-conspirator she was, but instead she was biting her lips, desperately trying to hold back tears. Happy tears, for sure.

She'd moved on admirably from the mess their parents had inflicted upon them. Now it was his turn.

By the end of the meeting, terms had been agreed upon in principle, with minor legalities to be worked out before anything was put in stone. When the board realised the possibilities the untying of the Bainbridge family knots afforded them, they were less shocked, and more excited. For the foundation, yes, but most unexpectedly for him.

Each and every one came up and shook his hand and thanked him for making it the powerhouse it was today.

'Your grandfather would be so proud,' said one of the elder statesmen who'd been on the board in his grandfather's time.

'He wouldn't be turning in his grave?' Dax asked with the closest thing to a smile he'd felt in days.

'Hell, no! If he'd managed to go another five years before the hours he bled into this place finally killed him, he would have done the same thing! You've got my vote on one condition.'

'Which is?'

'You'll consider donating in future.'

'Deal.'

Dax shook the man's hand and exited the boardroom, leaving Lauren to do the chit-chatting. The fact that he'd never be forced to schmooze in honour of the Bainbridge name was liberating.

Walking to the lift, as habit dictated he checked his mobile and found he'd had several missed calls. Clearly word was out already. He recognised some numbers as press, the competition, family, a couple of friends.

The lift opened at his arrival, like some kind of nod to it being the last time he left the building as its leader, and as the doors closed a name popped onto the screen that made his heart beat so hard against his chest he held a fist over the spot and took a long careful breath.

Caitlyn. She'd called only ten minutes earlier.

Blood pumping in his ears, he lifted the phone to his ear to listen to his messages, only to discover he had no service. He'd have to wait 'til the lift stopped. It took its sweet time to descend. So he waited, with his right leg twitching, all the way to the car park.

The second the door opened he exploded from the lift and the phone was at his ear as he stalked towards his car in the CEO's reserved spot.

It rang once, twice.

A gentle exhalation of breath slid softly through the phone, sliding through him like an elixir, warming his blood and ending up a coil of heat in his solar plexus. Then an all too familiar voice said, 'Dax.'

Okay, so he hadn't listened to the plethora of no doubt congratulatory messages first. They could wait. He told himself that calling her was like eating your vegetables before your dessert. Maybe she wanted her scarf back. Maybe she'd misdialled. Whatever she wanted, he was just getting it over with so he could enjoy the rest of his banner day.

'Caitlyn,' he said.

'Dax,' she said again as he slid behind the wheel of his car, shoving the phone into its hands-free slot. 'I'd like to see you if I could. There are…things I'd like to say.'

His hands gripped the leather steering wheel and his eyes closed tight. It had been more than a week since he'd last seen her, standing there in his kitchen, her hair gloriously dishevelled, her legs bare all the way to her thighs, her curves barely hidden beneath his old red T-shirt as it slipped slightly off one shoulder.

Yeah. Maybe it would be good to see her again in a

less evocative light. Maybe that was what he needed to get real closure.

He'd never had closure with his parents and it had eaten away at him for years. Giving this thing a clean ending would mean he could truly get on with his life.

He picked the time, later that evening. Enough for him to come down from the high of what he'd just given up so that he couldn't mistake one feeling for the other.

She chose the place. His eyes flew open in surprise.

He saw his reflection in the tinted windows. His hair not so neat as it usually was. Dark smudges beneath his eyes. His lips a thin slash across a weary face.

'Caitlyn,' he said as he revved the engine.

'Yes, Dax.'

'Bring the ring.'

CHAPTER ELEVEN

THE Sand Bar felt different so early in the evening. Quiet. Genteel even with the low conversation of the small after work crowd and smooth seventies R & B. Though Caitlyn's mood couldn't have been more dissimilar.

While earlier in the day she'd felt as if she were floating an inch off the ground—that was what getting rid of five years' worth of baggage in the form of extraneous bling would do for a girl—now she felt so uptight she could barely stand still.

She tugged at her snug little belted sweater dress, twisting it straight. She smoothed down her hair. Fiddled with her grandmother's earrings. She paced, her footsteps echoing on the recently polished floor, her watermelon-coloured toenails winking up at her hopefully.

She'd changed her outfit ten times before heading out again, needing a little extra oomph. Especially with the last words Dax had said to her jangling about inside her head.

Bring the ring.

Her fingers closed tightly around her enamel clutch purse with the ring reposing daintily inside as if she were waiting for a cat burglar to spring up from behind the bar and nab it from her. Not on her watch!

Her knees grew wobbly at the thought of giving it back. Not only because she thought it the most beautiful ring ever, but because, as she'd learned earlier that day, it would mark the real end of her relationship with Dax more than words flung in anger and disappointment ever could.

Bring the ring.

She shook Dax's voice from her head. This wasn't his party. It was hers. Her turn to say what she wanted to say, not what she thought she ought to out of the fear of losing all she loved. Thinking like that only destined her to be alone.

'Screw that!' she said to the chandelier over her head.

'Caitlyn?'

Dax. His name came to her on an inner sigh. She closed her eyes, mostly to hold back the tears that gathered there at the sound of his deep velvety voice. The voice of the man she loved.

She turned. He stood mere metres away. Grey suit, neat white shirt, pale striped tie. God, he was beautiful.

Beautiful, and in pain. She saw hurt in his eyes. He was wary of her. The mere scraps of confidence she was holding onto for dear life frayed away to dust.

He was a formidable man. Yet he was watching her as if he were preparing for a frontal attack. And for the first time that day she was truly fearful that she'd made such a mess of things that there was no repairing their relationship in any form. That after this meeting he would be gone from her life for ever.

But if she was her father's daughter at all, she wasn't going to take failure lying down. She'd had a false start, and a big one. But now she had a goal well and truly in mind, if there was any chance to mend what they had, no matter how slim that she might be, she was going to give it a red-hot go.

'Thanks for coming,' she said, plastering a smile on her

face. A ridiculous, incongruous smile. But it was either that or throw herself at him.

'You're welcome.'

The fact that they were being so polite considering the first time they'd met they'd traded verbal spars like pros almost brought Caitlyn down, but she marshalled her reserves and motioned to a pair of barstools. 'Would you care to sit down?'

The spot was public, open, making it less likely she would give into the growing desire to brush the stray lock of dark hair from his forehead.

Dax watched her for a mere moment more, his eyes unreadable, his back stiff, making her almost sob in relief when he slid off his suit jacket and threw it onto the bar, then loosened his tie and lowered himself to the stool.

He motioned to the bartender, gesturing to the nearest tap.

'Beer?' Caitlyn asked, nodding to the bartender that she'd have the same. She settled on the stool beside his, careful not to touch knees.

'Beer,' he said with a decisive nod, his long fingers playing with a cardboard coaster. The dark lock of hair curling down onto his forehead was so tempting she had to curl her fingernails into her palm. 'One of a long line of changes I'm making in my life.'

Caitlyn swallowed down the desperate need to know if she might have a chance at being one of them, or if she'd missed the boat for good.

Dax reached into his wallet to throw a note onto the bar that covered both drinks. Her heart twisted at the simple elegance of the move. 'I resigned my post at the foundation this afternoon.'

'You never!' she said, giving him a punch on the upper arm before she could stop herself.

She drew her fist back, shoving the offending appendage under her opposite arm. But it was done. His eyes slid to his arm, his forehead creasing before his mouth kicked up at one corner as he slid his wallet back into his jacket. 'I did.'

He hadn't looked at her, hadn't said a word about the contact, but she felt the warmth of him, and of that tiny flicker of a smile as if the ceiling had opened up and the midday sun was shining down atop her head.

She prayed to everything that was good and holy to give her a chance. To give them a chance. To help her find the right words to make him look at her again the way he'd just looked at his arm.

While Dax nodded his thanks at the bartender as he slid over the tall schooners of amber bubbles their way, Caitlyn said, 'You have been a busy boy.'

'I've had time to fill.' With that he tipped back the frothy glass, drawing her eyes to the workings of his throat.

'Yeah, me too.'

'Doing?' He glanced at her briefly, the familiar dark heat of his eyes making her stomach feel as if it were in free fall.

She looked down at her feet to hide her suddenly burning cheeks. 'I, ah, I got my toenails painted.'

Dax shifted his knees apart so that hers rested in the nook between, not touching, but trapped, and together they looked at her toes. She heard him breathe deep through his nostrils before they both looked up, gazes colliding.

You can not lose this man again.

With that thought bolstering her confidence just enough, she said, 'And now to our regularly scheduled programming. I know I don't hold much sway right now, but if I can just ask for you to hear me out, there are things I'd like to clarify. If I may.'

Dax put down his beer and breathed deep through his

nose, his inscrutable gaze not once leaving hers. His voice was extra deep as he said, 'I have nowhere else to be.'

Caitlyn clasped tight to her clutch, and she plunged in.

'That night when we first met I was going through some things. Dealing, badly, with mistakes I'd made. Relationship-type mistakes where I'd mistaken affection for love. Again and again and again.'

She paused to check his temperature, but apart from a gentle rise and fall of his chest he didn't move. She went on.

'And just as I'd decided I needed to change things up, there *you* were. Pure heaven in a dark grey suit. The very idea that a man like you could ever, ever, think himself in… in *love* with me—' she swallowed, the very word creating inconvenient fireworks inside her '—seemed as likely as discovering I'm half Martian.'

'Your mother's side,' Dax said without a pause.

Laughter shot from Caitlyn's mouth. Relief, hope, and fear flashed through her like disco lights—on off, mixing and fading, making her feel light-headed. Especially when he went back to frowning into his beer.

'Martian or not, I am my mother's daughter, and knowing how cold and bitter she became, and remained, after Dad died…' Her toes curled into her sandals. 'I always thought I gravitated to men who gave me the affection I'd been missing in my teens. But now I wonder if I chose guys I knew would never leave me as deeply heartbroken as Mum still is once they'd gone. Either. Both. Who knows?'

He rolled his shoulder before lifting his head, but Caitlyn glanced away at the last second, her pluck not extending quite far enough to bear looking Dax in the eye as she said, 'What I do know is that all that ended the day I met you.'

Her heart beat so hard she felt it bumping against her ribs and she could hear nothing of the sounds of the bar over the heavy whump whump whump of blood in her ears.

She closed her eyes, the words echoing as she said, 'I'm not proud of what I must have made you think the day we parted, Dax, but I want you to know that you were no accident. I sought you out. I wanted you because from the moment I touched you I knew you were different from any man I'd ever met.'

Her eyes flung open as his knees bumped hers. He'd flinched at her choice of words. Only she had no clue if she'd hit a sore spot, or good.

She breathed deep, and lifted her head to find herself captured by a pair of hot hazel eyes. Eyes that no longer looked quite so haunted. Eyes that held a glimmer of a smile.

God, but she loved him. Had loved him for weeks. Months. For ever. How could she not have known it sooner? None of that mattered. What mattered was she knew it now. And she wanted him to know it too.

When Dax's hand landed on her thigh her eyes zeroed in on it, not daring to hope. Then as his thumb passed soft circles over her knee the heat of his touch settled with a delicious deep thud at her very centre.

Inevitably, like a pendulum that had held far too long at the top of its arc, her eyes swung back to his.

'And then what happened?' Dax asked, sliding his hand another inch, the tips of his fingers finding their way beneath the hem of her skirt.

She breathed in and out. Not as if it helped. No man had ever managed to take her breath away quite as he did. 'I freaked out, of course! And then,' she said, 'I discovered to my constant chagrin that you weren't just some gorgeous guy in a suit and I freaked out just a little more.'

He raised an eyebrow.

'Fine,' she said, a smile tugging at the corners of her mouth, 'you are totally some gorgeous guy in a suit.'

He waved a hand over his face, as if she was embarrassing him. Laughter ruffled her insides, fresh and bracing, like breeze through a bird's feathers.

But she was not done yet.

'I'm basically a happy person, but *you* also know the bruises I hide below. The rough bits I assumed would only make it harder for someone to love me. You knew *me* and still you stayed. Then my freaking out took on gargantuan proportions.'

She held his gaze. He was smiling now. That slow, hot smile that meant he was thinking bad thoughts. Good bad thoughts, the kind that always boded so well for her.

She licked her lips, and said, 'All I can say is you're lucky you're so unfairly sexy. I mean, your fingers were built for sin. And that thing you do with your mouth…'

She shivered deliciously.

His fingers tightened on her thigh.

The tension arcing between them in that moment was vibrating so hard, if she'd wanted him back in her bed, she probably could have stopped there. But for the first time in her life she wanted more than a dazzling rush. She wanted everything.

She lay her hand over his, tucking her cool fingers around his warm ones, and waited until she had his full attention. Only then did she say, 'In the past, the idea of happily ever afters gave me palpitations, so when I found your ring… To me it represented the beginning of the end. And the thought of never seeing you again, of never feeling like this—'

She slid his hand an inch higher, feeling it tense as sensation shuddered through her at his touch. His eyes clouded over, dark and full of such desire her stomach curled in on itself in pure pleasure.

Her last words tumbled out of her in a mad rush. 'I've

missed you, Dax. Like crazy. Missed you with the kind of bone-deep ache I've spent my whole life avoiding. And then I realised there was only one sure way to avoid feeling that way. All I had to do was let go and let myself love you. So that's what I did.'

She stopped to take a breath. A deep one. One that shook through her middle and made her feel ever so slightly faint. But when Dax's fingers curled sure and tight around hers she knew the wait, the mistakes, every false start that had led to this point had been worth it.

She finished with a shrug because that was that. She had no idea what Dax was thinking as his eyes had left hers to rove over her face. All she could do was sit there, not faint, and hope that he loved what he saw.

Though, no. That wasn't all she could do. In fact…

She slid from the stool as elegantly as she could in her short skirt, then extricated herself from the circle of Dax's body, which was an achievement in itself considering how her body was urging her to do anything but.

Then she got down onto one knee and from her purse pulled the small velvet box, holding it out to him on one shaking hand.

'I'm sorry I went so crazy when I found this ring, and I'm sorry in advance that I can't promise I won't go crazy again at some point in the future. But that's what you get when you get me. I'm not easy and I'm not without occasional drama. But I hope that's half the reason why you want me. And I want you to want me. More than words can say. Because I'm head over heels, for ever and ever, in love with you, Dax Bainbridge.'

Dax looked down at her as if she were nuts, until realisation spread across his face. His eyes grew wide, his mouth slack. If she wasn't half wondering what slimy thing was that she had just knelt on, it might even have been funny.

Dax looked around in alarm, as if the gallantry police were about to nab him for letting her kneel there so long. Then with breathtaking strength he grabbed her by the elbows and picked her bodily up off the floor. Her feet landed on the wood with a clack of heels.

'What the hell do you think you're doing?' he asked, his eyes wide, his voice gruff.

'What does it look like?'

'No!' he said so loudly a handful of people at the other end of the bar turned and stared. Caitlyn shot them a half-smile to show everything was okay, even while she had no idea if it was.

Oh, God, had she misread him so completely? She really was *such* a screw-up at this relationship stuff! How could she have hoped to have gone from relationship idiot to savant in a day? Reading the creases in his forehead, the flickers in his eyes, as if she really had a single clue—

Then he was holding out his hand, looking at the ring. He'd asked her to bring it, and now she was about to find out why.

She passed it to him, putting her future in his hands. Literally. It was one of the more petrifying moments of her life, even though they really were such lovely hands.

Enough people had seen what she'd done that they now had a small audience. Noticing the gawkers, Dax swore beneath his breath, then grabbed her by the hand and led her to the dance floor, which was half full with slow-dancing couples.

'Did I screw everything up again?' she asked, as she clacked behind him.

'You've said your piece and, before you do anything crazy, I want to say mine,' he said, his voice tight. 'Fair?'

She nodded.

He wrapped his arms wrapped around her, pulling her close. She slid a hand into his and put the other over his heart, which was thumping so hard she could feel it through his shirt.

'Caitlyn.'

'Mmm-hmm,' she mumbled.

'Look at me.'

She did as she was told, looking up at dark eyes, dark hair, dark expression. The first time she'd seen him she'd thought him untouchable. This time she reached up and brushed the lock of hair from his forehead, her fingers tingling as they caressed his warm, oh, so touchable skin.

A muscle worked in his cheek and he pulled her tighter still, the feel of his hard thighs pressing against her taking her breath away.

Then he said, 'No more freaking out, okay?'

She shook her head, no.

'Good, because these past few days have been pure hell. I had to give up the family company just to find something to take my mind off you. I don't want to go through that again. And for that I have to see you every day. To talk to you whenever I need to. To touch you whenever I want to. To kiss you every chance I get. To make love to you as many times a day as humanly possible. To hold you every night for the rest of my life. And I'm willing to do whatever it takes to make that happen. Marry you, not marry you. Give you a ring, give you an island. Adopt a rescue llama, adopt Franny. Whatever it takes.'

He put a finger beneath her chin and lifted her head so that she could see the absolute sincerity deep within his dark eyes.

And there she saw the depth of his love for her and she understood it completely. And by the smile that slowly

beamed across his gorgeous face she could only imagine
how bright the love inside her was shining too.

'Forgive me?' she said, her voice shaky.

'For what?'

'For saying yes to other men and not meaning it.'

'Sweetheart, if you had any idea how glad I am you
didn't mean it with them you wouldn't look so concerned
right about now.'

He tilted her chin a fraction higher as he leant to press
his lips to hers. It felt as if it had been weeks, months, a
lifetime, since she'd kissed him as an explosion of sensation burst inside her. His kiss melted away any last doubt
she might yet have harboured as to his absolute sincerity,
or her own.

She slid her hands into his hair, stood on tiptoes and
kissed him back with all her might. The music stopped, or
maybe it hadn't. She couldn't hear anything over the ram-
pant beating of her own heart. Or was that his?

When his lips left hers she felt as if she were floating a
foot from the ground, as if the weight that had borne down
upon her shoulders all her life was finally gone.

She was loved. Truly, honestly, deeply loved. And she
loved someone just as much. It was nothing like she'd even
imagined it could feel. More exhilarating. It was a high she
knew she'd never get used to, never take for granted. And
she had one beautiful man to thank for it all.

The music started up again and she slowly lowered herself back to the ground, sliding down his body as if parting
from it for even half a beat was too much to bear.

'So what do you say to my fine print?' he asked.

'Fine by me,' she said, running a greedy hand across
his broad shoulders.

'Which parts?'

'The island. The llama. You.'

He relaxed and then she realised how nervous he'd been about his own declaration. Wow. It only made her love him more.

She sank against him, limp, warm, happy. And best of all he let her.

'You do realise I am officially unemployed,' he said, his lips resting on the top of her head.

'We'll be fine.' She sighed into his strong chest. 'I have a good job.'

She felt him pause a moment, and knew—now that she was more sure of her abilities at reading him—the hesitation amounted to how best to tell her his niftiness with finance had made him worth a mint all on his own. Caitlyn, of course, knew already. Franny. Google.

She casually slid a hand over his backside and back up to his shoulders again. 'Will you be okay covering your rent?'

'Why?' he asked, his voice now a growl. 'Are you offering to help out?'

'Sure,' she murmured, her fingers now playing with the warm skin exposed by his open collar. 'My bed's big enough for two, which we've proven admirably. And Franny is a fairly quiet housemate, most of the time.'

His laughter rumbled through her. 'Not going to happen in a thousand years.'

She smiled from the tips of her highlights to her delighted watermelon toenails. 'Oh, well. It was a fun thought while it lasted.'

He wrapped his arms about her waist and slid her against his hardness, which was getting harder by the second. 'How's this for fun? Move in with me.'

'Okay.' She sighed into him, rocking in rhythm with the music while her hands roved over his gorgeous chest, his strong back, his hard stomach, the cold bump of his belt buckle.

'That was easier than expected.'

'You seem to have found me in a strangely good mood.'

'I see that. And I intend on taking complete advantage.'

'Go right ahead,' she said, closing her eyes as she leaned against his chest, his heartbeat thumping gently against her temple. 'What do you want? A good deal on a Z9? Done. Anything else?'

He stopped rocking. She stumbled, her loose limbs taking a moment to catch up with the news. She held his lapels and dragged her blissfully woozy head upright to frown at him.

His hand slipped to her chin, holding it still as he looked deep into her eyes.

'Marry me.'

The words tickled at old wounds, and she braced herself for the merest glimmer of fear, but instead she heard nothing but the smooth tripping beat of Stevie Wonder singing 'Do I Do'.

Something glinted in the corner of her gaze. The ring. Her ring.

'Yes,' she said, never more certain of anything in her whole life.

He slipped the flower of diamonds onto her finger. It looked exactly how she felt, full of delight and sparkle and vivacity.

She held the ring to her ears. Her grandmother's earrings, glass chandeliers with tiny flowers at the clasps that she'd picked out with her dad all those years ago from a dime store for her entire life savings of nine dollars and fifty cents, swung softly against her neck. 'They match.'

He nodded. 'I know.'

Of course he knew. He knew where she came from and

had every intention of being right beside her wherever she was going.

Beautiful Dax Bainbridge and she—a perfect matching set.

* * * * *

REQUEST YOUR FREE BOOKS!

2 FREE NOVELS PLUS
2 FREE GIFTS!

YES! Please send me 2 FREE Harlequin Presents® novels and my 2 FREE gifts (gifts are worth about $10). After receiving them, if I don't wish to receive any more books, I can return the shipping statement marked "cancel." If I don't cancel, I will receive 6 brand-new novels every month and be billed just $4.30 per book in the U.S. or $4.99 per book in Canada. That's a saving of at least 14% off the cover price! It's quite a bargain! Shipping and handling is just 50¢ per book in the U.S. and 75¢ per book in Canada.* I understand that accepting the 2 free books and gifts places me under no obligation to buy anything. I can always return a shipment and cancel at any time. Even if I never buy another book, the two free books and gifts are mine to keep forever.

106/306 HDN FERQ

Name _____ (PLEASE PRINT)

Address _____ Apt. #

City _____ State/Prov. _____ Zip/Postal Code

Signature (if under 18, a parent or guardian must sign)

Mail to the **Reader Service:**
IN U.S.A.: P.O. Box 1867, Buffalo, NY 14240-1867
IN CANADA: P.O. Box 609, Fort Erie, Ontario L2A 5X3

Not valid for current subscribers to Harlequin Presents books.

**Are you a current subscriber to Harlequin Presents books
and want to receive the larger-print edition?
Call 1-800-873-8635 or visit www.ReaderService.com.**

* Terms and prices subject to change without notice. Prices do not include applicable taxes. Sales tax applicable in N.Y. Canadian residents will be charged applicable taxes. Offer not valid in Quebec. This offer is limited to one order per household. All orders subject to credit approval. Credit or debit balances in a customer's account(s) may be offset by any other outstanding balance owed by or to the customer. Please allow 4 to 6 weeks for delivery. Offer available while quantities last.

Your Privacy—The Reader Service is committed to protecting your privacy. Our Privacy Policy is available online at www.ReaderService.com or upon request from the Reader Service.

We make a portion of our mailing list available to reputable third parties that offer products we believe may interest you. If you prefer that we not exchange your name with third parties, or if you wish to clarify or modify your communication preferences, please visit us at www.ReaderService.com/consumerschoice or write to us at Reader Service Preference Service, P.O. Box 9062, Buffalo, NY 14269. Include your complete name and address.

It all starts with a kiss

COMING JAN 22!

Check out the new Harlequin series.
Fun, flirty and sensual romances.

www.Harlequin.com